Body of Water

Body of Water

Daniel J. Boyne

LYONS
PRESS

Essex, Connecticut

LP
LYONS PRESS

An imprint of Globe Pequot, the trade division of
The Rowman & Littlefield Publishing Group, Inc.
4501 Forbes Blvd., Ste. 200
Lanham, MD 20706
www.rowman.com

Distributed by NATIONAL BOOK NETWORK

British Library Cataloguing in Publication Information available

Library of Congress Cataloging-in-Publication Data

Names: Boyne, Daniel J., author.
Title: Body of water : a novel / Daniel J. Boyne.
Description: Essex, Connecticut : Lyons Press, [2023] | Summary: "Harvard
   University rowing coach and long-time crew luminary Dan Boyne tells a tale of
   murder on the Charles River in Cambridge, MA. A wealthy man is murdered,
   and there are plenty of suspects within the rowing community in Cambridge"—
   Provided by publisher.
Identifiers: LCCN 2022040826 (print) | LCCN 2022040827 (ebook) |
   ISBN 9781493071210 (cloth ; alk. paper) | ISBN 9781493071227 (epub)
Subjects: LCSH: Harvard University—Rowing—Fiction. | LCGFT: Thrillers
   (Fiction). | Novels.
Classification: LCC PS3602.O977 B63 2023 (print) | LCC PS3602.O977
   (ebook) | DDC 813/.6—dc23/eng/20221028
LC record available at https://lccn.loc.gov/2022040826
LC ebook record available at https://lccn.loc.gov/2022040827

♾™ The paper used in this publication meets the minimum requirements of
American National Standard for Information Sciences—Permanence of Paper for
Printed Library Materials, ANSI/NISO Z39.48-1992.

To my wife, Karen

Acknowledgments

$\mathcal{I}$'d like to thank Seamus Kent of the Massachusetts state police department and Lieutenant Robert Harrington of the Harvard campus police department for helping me out with various questions about police protocol, interview techniques, and modern technology. I'd also like to thank Ed Hewitt, the dogged editor of row2k.com, who published the early chapters of this novel on his world-famous website. I would also like to thank Margot Mayor, a complete stranger, who started reading these online chapters and stepped forward to graciously volunteer to be an editor, along with my wife, Karen; Gail Caldwell, my dear friend and fellow writer, who lent her critical eye to the final draft of the book; Will Schmitt, my medical advisor; and Kit Buckley, my IT specialist. Lastly, but not least, a big thank you to Gene Brissie and Rick Rinehart at the Lyons Press for their support over the years with my writing endeavors. All these people helped *Body of Water* come into being.

"Loss is the price we pay for progress," she said. "Only as we leave things behind do we move forward."

—Robert B. Parker, *Painted Ladies*

· 1 ·

Downstream

"*Big* Ed" Masterson shoved off from the Cambridge Boat Club dock and just sat there for a second, gazing at the half-lit sky and the still waters of the Charles. It was going to be a perfect day, one of those rare October mornings when there was a slight chill in the air, soon remedied by several minutes of hard rowing. He took a few strokes, first with his arms and back, and then with the accompaniment of his sizable legs. He loved sculling, because it utilized every piece of his 6'5" body, which often seemed awkward and clumsy on dry land but never so on water.

He'd barely made it to the Eliot Bridge when he heard the unmistakable *thunk* of something hitting the bow of his hand-built wooden single, crafted by the Australian boatwright Grahame King. He stopped abruptly and gazed down into the dark water. It was barely dawn, a few days after the Head of the Charles Regatta, and there was still a lot of debris strewn about the surface of the water from weekend revelers. The annual rowing competition in Boston was like a huge tailgate party for those involved with the sport, and hundreds of spectators lined the banks of the river to watch the endless parade of boats go by.

It took his 55-year-old, sun-stricken eyes a few moments to finally spot the blue Igloo cooler, floating just below the surface. He swore briefly as he fished it out of the water and then heaved it toward the Cambridge shore with one arm, where it landed with a dull thud in front of the VFW post, just upstream of the bridge. Then he wiped his hands on his cotton T-shirt and started rowing again.

Rowing was his primary obsession in life, and he was compulsive about it. Anything that got in the way of his daily rendezvous with the river bothered him, perhaps more than it should have. And now in Masterson's mind, a full minute of water time had already been wasted. More important than that, one piece of trash meant that there was probably going to be others. Suddenly, his sacred morning row had been defiled, and he had to stop himself from descending into a bad mood. *Shake it off*, he told himself, gripping his oars tighter. A hard row could still fix everything. But if anything or anyone else got in his way, he would curse at them too—man, woman, or child. He didn't care, although he probably should have, for he had coached at Harvard University long enough that his name was forever connected to that institution, and would reflect poorly on it, even though he was no longer working there.

"Okay, okay," he whispered out loud.

He took several more strokes to get clear of the Eliot Bridge, then spun his boat around and headed downstream toward the starting line of the world-famous regatta. His plan was to do a practice piece for time over the 3.1-mile course, just to see if he could better the time he'd done a few days ago, when another competitor had unfortunately cut him off during the race, slowing him down and ruining his chances of winning. Pulling hard on port, he drew his boat around the sharp turn, hugging the Boston shore, where he spotted a few summer drifters sleeping along the wooded bank. Soon it would be too cold for them to stay outdoors, sleeping bags or not. Briefly, he wondered where they might go—Florida, perhaps, or maybe Mexico. In his youth, Masterson had favored a more nomadic lifestyle, and a part of him still missed it, settled now in Boston with the Charles River as his primary connection to nature.

As the Eliot Bridge disappeared from his view, he briefly tried to imagine what the river had been like over a 100 years ago, based on some images from a book he'd been reading about the history of the bucolic waterway. The old black-and-white photographs depicted a radically different body of water than the one that he currently rowed on. It was hard to believe that the lower stretch of nearly still water, now adorned with architecturally wrought bridges and green parklands, had once been a sewage-filled tidal concourse, rising and falling over nine feet before it emptied into Boston Harbor.

As Masterson headed further downstream, he noticed that the water table was high enough now that some water would soon have to be released from the dam downstream, behind the Museum of Science. The dam not only kept the river levels in check but also helped control the overall water quality of the Charles, preventing seawater from entering. Boats could still come and go, of course, and once while he was coaching at Harvard, Masterson had taken a crew all the way out into the harbor on a 20-mile excursion that roughly followed the route of a ferry service the university had run long ago. There was a fish ladder, too, which let migrating species enter the river and swim upstream to spawn. In late spring, the rocky shallows along the edges of the Charles would be boiling with hundreds of blue-backed herring and alewives.

Passing by Newell, the Harvard University men's boathouse, he felt the sun settle onto his back, keeping his sweat from cooling. Then he noticed a couple of freshman crews putting their boats in the water.

"Bastards," he muttered, under his breath.

Until a few years ago, it had been his job to coach the Harvard fourth and fifth boat heavyweight crews, under the watchful eye of head coach Harry Parker. At first, things had gone quite well, and Masterson's rough-around-the-edges, Philadelphia style of coaching had worked in perfect complement to Parker's laconic, patrician delivery. Eventually, however, Parker had let Masterson go after several seasons of mixed results, culminating in a screaming match with a freshman coxswain named Finley Sparks.

Sparks was a legacy recruit, the son of a famous Harvard oarsman named Sheldon Sparks, and he had come to the university with a chip on his shoulder and a need to prove his superior intellect. He did this primarily by mocking everything and everyone, including coach Masterson and his blue-collar background. In Masterson's mind, Sparks was just a little guy with a big mouth. One day on the water, he told him so, along with a few other choice comments. Masterson had been dismissed, while Sparks had gone on to graduate and then make millions from a video game app he created during his senior year.

Masterson didn't care to dwell on that experience right now, so he picked up speed and passed skillfully under Anderson Bridge, which connected Harvard to its football stadium, trying to row away from the view and all the memories associated with it. He didn't really blame anyone but himself, but the problem with rowing was that you always looked backward. You couldn't help but regret all the bad strokes you had taken, and the poor steering that came from being blind to what lay ahead.

Because of his dismissal from Harvard, Masterson had initially been denied membership by every private rowing club on the Charles River, even CRI, the community boating facility which was supposedly open to all. For a while he just kept his boat on top of his pickup truck and drove up to Watertown every morning to launch from the public dock there. Pissed off, he had a T-shirt printed up by a friend of his in Harvard Square that said SYRC with crossed oars on the front and "Screw You Rowing Club" on the back. He still wore the T-shirt, even after a few of his buddies finally got him into the Cambridge Boat Club, vouching for his character and denying the rumors that he was an irascible cuss from Philly who couldn't keep his mouth shut whenever he got mad.

In figure and form, Ed Masterson looked a little like Jack Kelly Sr., the famous Philadelphia sculler whose bronze statue still guarded the banks of the Schuylkill River. He had overly long legs and arms, a decent physique, and a devilish way of toying with his rivals. The latter technique he had learned from Parker, his former boss, who always got even if someone beat him. Out on the river, this trait played out in various ways. Masterson would often slow down if another sculler was trailing him, letting the man or woman catch up a bit and even start to pass him, then he would take ten hard strokes and slip away. He would then slow down again, giving the other sculler false encouragement, and the cat-and-mouse game would be repeated for as long as possible. Older scullers on the Charles knew enough not to get caught up in it, but there were plenty of young ones still left to torture, scattered about the Charles River like bits of flotsam and jetsam.

A tin can hit his bow, and he swore again.

* * * * *

Masterson took 10 hard strokes and then 10 easy, then 20 on and 20 off. The heart rate monitor that was cinched around his chest beeped rapidly and then settled down again as he went through this cyclical warm up. It steadily tracked higher with the longer duration of hard strokes—150, 160, 170, 180. He kept a watchful eye on it; he had to be careful these days.

Last spring, he'd had a big scare out on the river when his heart suddenly started racing out of control, upwards of 220 beats a minute. He stopped rowing, shaken, and then spent several minutes in a fetal position, trying not to capsize, as he hunched over his oars and let his boat drift aimlessly downstream. He had no idea what was happening, but it felt like a panic attack. When his heart rate finally settled down, he paddled home, pale faced and shaken, and then sat on the dock for several minutes. He chatted with a few of his rowing buddies at the club to try and sort out what had gone wrong.

A few days later he was navigating his way through a maze of corridors and elevators at Massachusetts General Hospital, trying to locate the sports cardiology office. When he finally found it, arriving ten minutes late, an impatient young tech named Donald quickly ushered him into a small room filled with the hum and buzz of electrified machinery. He was instructed to remove his shirt, then he stood still as his chest was plastered with electrodes. Donald then placed a clamp over his nose and fit a clumsy respirator over his mouth. Masterson allowed all of this to be done to him and then sat on a rowing machine and watched as another tech calibrated a monitoring screen. The contraption would apparently provide heart rate, breath volume, and blood pressure data. As he sat there, waiting for the go-ahead to begin rowing, Masterson suddenly realized that Donald looked remarkably like Finley Sparks, who'd once told him, "My dad can probably buy you out of a job." Masterson had laughed at the arrogant boy at the time, dismissing his comment as an empty boast. In the end, however, the joke was on him.

After ten minutes on the rowing machine, which left Masterson lacquered in sweat, the respirator and nose clamp were promptly removed. The second tech also pulled the electrodes off his chest and told him he could put his shirt back on. Then Donald abruptly left the room. Several minutes passed, and there was still no sign of the cardiologist. Masterson was chilled from the air-conditioned room, and he found the loud hum of machinery and the long wait unnerving. He was used to doing pieces competitively, and all he really cared about was whether he had beaten any of the other patients who had tested before him. Donald could have at least revealed that information, Masterson thought. He stood up and paced the room, studying the signed photographs of various sports celebrities who had been former patients prominently displayed on the walls. There was an ice hockey player from the Boston Bruins, a few Olympic runners, and even a soccer player he hadn't heard of before. Just as he was about to leave the room and sneak out of the hospital, the chief cardiologist came in, introducing himself as Dr. Hamish.

"So, to cut to the chase, Edward, you have atrial fib," he said calmly. "It's not uncommon among elite oarsmen still rowing competitively into their 40s and 50s."

"Well, that's reassuring," Masterson laughed. "Good to know I'm among the elite."

"See these heart rate spikes?" Dr. Hamish asked, smiling politely and pointing to a paper printout.

Masterson nodded, even though he really didn't know what he was looking at.

"Most people show a steady rise in heart rate and blood pressure. Yours is spike-y."

Spike-y, he thought. Was that a medical term?

"So, what do I do about it?" he asked, trying to remain calm.

"There are essentially two options," Hamish said. "You can try to control it with medication, or we can try an ablation."

"An ablation?" he said, raising his eyebrows. "That sounds like a Catholic rite."

Dr. Hamish laughed amiably. "Slightly different. We essentially try to cauterize the cardiac tissue that is sending false information to your heart, so it won't randomly start to race out of control."

"Seems a bit barbaric," Masterson quipped. Some of the guys at CBC had mentioned this procedure to him, however, so he was already aware of this radical option.

"I'll send you some information to look over. Then we can talk again."

Masterson nodded, suddenly irritated by the doctor's casual manner. "Have you ever been hooked up to this machine, Doc?" he asked.

Hamish smiled and shook his head.

"Really?" he said, lifting his eyebrows. "Why not?"

The cardiologist shrugged. "I suppose I don't really want to know my pathetic level of fitness."

Masterson nodded, then pressed the younger man further. "Just out of curiosity—when was the last time you went to a doctor?"

Dr. Hamish grinned again, as he made his way out the door. "Oh, I don't go to doctors anymore," he laughed.

"Great," Masterson muttered under his breath. "I'm being seen by a guy who doesn't believe in the medical system."

* * * * *

After his visit to MGH, Masterson did some research on the web and simply upped his intake of potassium. It seemed to keep his racing heart in check. Still, he was a bit more careful now out on the river. Several years earlier, he had heard of an older sculler at the Cambridge Boat Club who'd blacked out during a race while pushing himself too hard. The 70-year-old had capsized and drowned, suspended upside down underwater for several minutes before the umpire launch had rescued him. Several CBC members had gone to the funeral and spoken during the eulogy, trying to honor their rowing comrade's passing by offering up the fact that he had "died with his boots on," but the family didn't buy this rowing romanticism, and neither did Masterson. He never wanted to go out that way.

Just before the Western Avenue bridge, he stopped briefly to adjust the rearview mirror clipped to his cap. Then he looked over at the old electric power plant building that had once been occupied by the Ford Motor Company. The ghosted logo was still visible on its brick façade. On some mornings now, his body felt like an old pickup truck—still strong but suffering from a creaky and loose suspension. Come to think of it, his transmission wasn't all that great either. His hips and shoulders often protested when he got out of bed in the morning, and he was even aware of the less than smooth running of his thoughts. Sometimes his memory seemed to skip over a few essential pieces that connected a train of thought—or lose track of them completely—turning it into a more abstract, dreamlike jumble. Being a rower, Masterson preferred to think of his mind as simply being more fluid now, rather than "janky," a word the Harvard boatman Charlie Abbott often used to describe machinery that didn't work so well.

But he could still row.

He started up again, trying to beat the Riverside scullers who were just launching from their dock to head down to the starting line of the racecourse. They dispersed out onto the river, like a swarm of mosquitos, and he didn't want to tangle with them today. Most of them liked to row against each other, and Masterson preferred to row alone. He certainly didn't want to bump into Anne Billings, an older female sculler he'd recently gone on a date with and then hadn't called back. As he rowed past Riverside Boat Club, he suddenly spotted her on the dock, waving to him. He picked up his pace and pretended not to notice her, knowing that if he saw her in person again, he could always blame it on bad eyesight. The rowing community on the Charles River was an incestuous cult, and you had to be careful about whom you hung out with off the water.

Passing under the railroad bridge, he took 20 more hard strokes at race pace as a final bit of warm-up. Then he stopped and spun around just below the Boston University boathouse, crossing the river to the Cambridge side and pointing his bow back upstream. He stopped for a minute, cradling his oar handles in his lap and laying his blades flat on the water for balance. Then he pulled off his extra shirt and wedged it into the tiny cockpit space that lay just in front of his feet. Looking astern, he spotted some team boats approaching from a distance, coming up fast from MIT, so he set the timer to zero, and without further ceremony launched into the three-mile piece.

When Masterson rowed hard, he didn't think about anything else other than keeping the boat balanced and moving constantly. He could feel when things were going well, and he didn't need any electronic gadgets to confirm this. Most of the younger scullers he knew were addicted to technology, but Masterson had learned the old way from the veteran scullers in Philadelphia. Instead of fixating on numerical data, these guys had taught him how to watch the rise and fall of the stern, the run of the boat, and the spacing of the oar puddles between strokes. Their voices were now permanently embedded in his brain, coaching him from within. Deep down, it wasn't the numbers on the stroke coach that inspired you but the way the boat felt when it began to "sing," the musical sound of water flowing under the hull.

Roughly a mile into the course, he passed Riverside Boat Club again. He could sense the younger scullers watching him, measuring his speed and power in their minds. Everyone on the river was a competitive son-of-a-bitch, whether they admitted it or not. He was going well now at 30 strokes a minute, and he'd just made it to the first mile marker in 6:25 when the bow of his wooden single hit something big.

"God damn it!" he shouted and instinctively checked his oars in the water, momentarily bracing the boat so as not to capsize. Just behind him he spotted the offending bit of flotsam—an oddly shaped object that slowly bobbed back up to the surface. There was something weird about the way it moved, rolling over like a lazy manatee. Suddenly he understood why, as the image registered in his brain. Then he started rowing away from it like a madman.

Unbelievable, he thought. *It couldn't be.*

He hit 33 strokes per minute, then 34. Full of adrenaline and raw fear, he continued to push himself along at that pace, heading straight up the "powerhouse" section of the river, past the old Ford factory on the Cambridge shore and the new Genzyme building on the Boston side, then through the Western Avenue bridge. Only once more did he have to alter his course, as he overtook a slower sculler who was out for a pleasure row, just beyond the Weeks Footbridge.

"Open your eyes!" he shouted angrily.

With one mile left, he was already gasping for breath. The cool air burned at the back of his throat as he tried to suck more oxygen into his lungs. Still, he pushed himself harder, moving by the Harvard boathouse and making doubly sure he didn't slow down there. His turn through the center arch of the Eliot Bridge was nearly perfect, and then he hugged the Cambridge shore going into the final push. Two minutes to go. The dull throb in the pit of his stomach had steadily begun to grow into a sickening gut punch, so he began to count strokes to take his mind off the pain, knowing that only 50 remained.

". . . 45, 46, 47 . . ."

When the bow of his boat crossed the finish line, he stopped rowing abruptly and collapsed over his oars. The boat continued to glide forward until it finally came to rest. For a while, he just sat there, lungs heaving, trying not to lose his balance. Eventually he looked down at his timing device, curious as to what this painful effort had produced. The LED readout of the stroke coach showed a 19:30—his fastest time to date. *Well, that was interesting*, he thought. *That was really something*.

He tried to do some simple arithmetic in his head, calculating his 500-meter split time average and comparing it against his stroke rating. He was trying to focus on something other than the image that kept popping into his brain. *Shake it off*, he told himself again. *It's not possible*. But suddenly he could no longer block it out. He leaned over the gunnels and threw up. Still dry heaving, he gazed down into the water, looking down at his own reflection. Then he let himself remember the face that he'd seen moments ago, looking up at him from just below the surface. Although the body had already begun to decompose, there was no mistaking its identity.

It was the ex-Harvard coxswain, Finley Sparks.

· 2 ·

Rules of the River

"So let me get this straight," the state trooper said. "You saw a body floating in the water, somewhere upstream of here . . . *and then you kept on rowing?*"

"Um, yes," Masterson replied, knitting his oversized eyebrows together. He looked down at the fallen leaves in the Magazine Beach parking lot as if studying the pieces of an incomprehensible puzzle, desperately trying to remember the detective's name. *Was it Clancy? Figgins?* The detective looked at him, waiting for a better reply.

"Well, I was right in the middle of a race piece . . ." Masterson started to explain, then realized this explanation didn't sound very good, especially to a nonrower. "I guess part of me couldn't believe what I just saw," he added. He looked up and gave the younger man an unconvincing smile. *Delaney. That was it!*

"Okay," the detective said, adding some notes to the contact information he'd already written down.

Sean Delaney was in his late 30s, with dark hair and an easygoing manner. He looked and acted nothing like what Masterson imagined a detective should. Admittedly, Masterson's knowledge of cops was largely based on TV shows and books like *Inspector Poirot* and *Spenser for Hire*, where the main character was generally a tortured soul with a substance abuse problem, at least one nervous tic, and an inability to hold onto long-term relationships. The guy standing in front of him, however, seemed perfectly normal. The sergeant was clean-cut and extremely polite. He had a handsome Irish face that looked remarkably like Masterson's favorite quarterback, Tom Brady.

"But you think you may have recognized the deceased?" Delaney prompted, ignoring the last disclaimer.

"I think so. I mean, it looked a lot like a coxswain I used to coach."

"Coxswain?"

"That's the guy who steers the boat."

"Right," Delaney nodded. "Do you remember his name?"

"Finley Sparks." *I'll never forget that one*, he thought to himself.

Delaney looked up and lifted his eyebrows, as if the same thought had just occurred to him. The victim's name sounded like something you'd expect for a rodeo clown, not a college boy.

"So, what happens now?" Masterson asked, giving a nervous sigh of relief now that the interview seemed to be over.

As if on cue, a posse of Ford SUVs began to pile into the dirt parking lot behind them. In addition to a Cambridge police unit, there was a car from Suffolk County sheriff's office, followed by another from Middlesex County. Next came a squad car from the Harvard University Police. Far off in the distance, they could hear the siren of a fire truck, slowly making its way down Memorial Drive through rush hour traffic.

"Well, first we have to find the corpse and retrieve it from the river," Delaney stated, glancing over his shoulder at the assembly of vehicles gathering behind him. The way he said it made it seem like there might be a problem. The Harvard police officer had already gotten out of his car and was making his way toward them, walking with the slow, measured gate of an older guy who still knew how to take care of himself. "Then the medical examiner will take the body to the morgue to do an autopsy and determine the cause of death." He nodded toward a jet-black medical examiner's truck, which had just pulled into the parking lot.

"Is it usually pretty obvious?" Masterson asked.

Delaney nodded. "Usually. Most of the time these things are accidental or self-inflicted."

Masterson noticed how he avoided the word *suicide*.

"Why all the different squad cars?" Masterson pressed.

Delaney gave him a quiet, patient look, without answering the question right away.

"It's a matter of sorting out jurisdiction," he finally said, just as the Harvard policeman closed the gap between them. "In general, the entire Charles River and the DCR parkland is considered state police territory, but we often have to work with either the Middlesex or Suffolk County DA's office—depending on which side of the river the body washes up on and if anything looks suspicious. I'm not sure why the Harvard campus police are here, but they may have gotten a courtesy call from the 911 dispatcher if you mentioned that a Harvard student was involved."

"Nice to see you too, Sean," said the Harvard cop, now standing right beside them. He looked to be about 60 years old, with gray-white hair and a round, grizzled face that had missed a day or two of shaving. Despite his age he was powerfully built, and when he shook hands with Masterson, he nearly took his hand off.

"Bob Rousseau," he said. "Didn't we meet a few years ago at the Newell boathouse?"

"Maybe," Masterson smiled, trying to remember the occasion. It might have been an alumni event or a police detail for the Head of the Charles.

"Lieutenant Rousseau," Delaney nodded, acknowledging the other policeman's rank. He lifted a pair of binoculars up to his eyes and began to scan the river in front of them.

"So, we have a missing Harvard student, possibly drowned?"

"Ex-Harvard student," Delaney corrected. It had been two years since Sparks had graduated.

"We're still interested," the Harvard cop said.

"And we have primary jurisdiction on DCR parkland," Delaney reiterated, still scanning the Charles River with the field glasses. "You're a little far afield, Bob."

"Perhaps," Rousseau replied, smiling. "Did you know that this was the site of the original Harvard Boathouse, built around 1898?"

"Nice fun fact," Delaney said. "But it doesn't change anything. You're still out of bounds."

"Don't worry, Sean," Rousseau said. "Your guys can collect the O.T."

"I'm with H Division," Delaney shot back.

Rousseau was still grinning. "And how is F Division doing? Or should I say F Troop?"

"Still under investigation," Delaney said. "I had nothing to do with that, and you know it."

"Of course," the Harvard policeman said.

While the two men bantered about insider gossip, Masterson wandered over to the grassy hummock where the armory stood. The old stone fortress now served as a maintenance shed for city lawn mowers and snow removal equipment, but it afforded one of the best views of the river. He studied the gray palate of the Charles from the higher vantage point. The sun had risen higher over the city skyline and the Prudential Center building, and it lit the gray water, turning it icy blue. Automatically, his eyes began to track along an imaginary line off the small promontory, where any smart coxswain or crew would start to align themselves with the middle of the river. Short-range, Masterson's vision was poor, but from a distance he could spot things that most people could not.

"Look. Over there!" he shouted.

Both men came over and tried to see where he was pointing. Delaney used his binoculars to get a better look and then politely handed them over to Rousseau.

Even without the field glasses, Masterson could now see Finley's old Harvard crew splash jacket, crimson colored, like a red splotch on a gray-blue canvas. A sea breeze had come up and it billowed the jacket full of air, making it even easier to spot.

A Boston Police Department and a Cambridge cop both came up and stood beside Delaney and Rousseau.

"Cordon this area off," Delaney instructed them. "We don't want a fairground here."

"Looks like wind is blowing it over to Cambridge," said the cop from the Suffolk Country Sherriff's office, smiling.

"Maybe not," said the guy from Middlesex. "The current may pull it back the other direction."

"Relax, gentlemen, I have a marine unit already on their way," Delaney said.

He turned away and spoke into a hand-held radio, and a crackly response came right back. Within seconds, a Boston Whaler with twin outboard engines came blasting through the Boston University Bridge, trailing a massive wake. The bridge was peppered with graffiti from college crews and townies alike.

Masterson had passed under it countless times, both out coaching and in his single scull, but today every detail around him was sharp, including the colors of the leaves under the surface of the shallow water. He felt his blood pumping through his veins and the way the cool October air had begun to freeze the exposed parts of his face and hands.

Within minutes, the marine unit had collected the body and towed it over toward them. Closer to the bridge, two guys in white jumpsuits and rubber gloves from the medical examiner's office then retrieved the body and began to place it into a body bag. The operation was made more difficult because Finley's right arm was raised over his head, and it couldn't be brought back to his side because of rigor mortis.

The odd way the arm was positioned, and the gray pallor of the corpse's face, made it look like a ghoulish Statue of Liberty. Finally, the two men just hauled Finley away on a gurney.

The entire procedure took several minutes, and as the body was being removed, Masterson just stood there, transfixed, not wanting to look but looking anyway. After the dead body disappeared into the ambulance, he could hear the flock of white geese that lived on the other side of the bridge, honking loudly as if they knew that something happened.

"Can you believe people used to swim here once?" Rousseau said, sidling up next to him.

Masterson didn't respond. He felt a familiar, uncomfortable sensation welling up inside him.

"I think I'm getting hypothermia," he said.

"C'mon, let's go. I'll give you a ride back to campus," Rousseau said.

"Okay if we leave, inspector?" he called out to Delaney, who waived back signaling that he'd call him later.

On the way to the car, Masterson paused briefly behind a bush to vomit. Rousseau said nothing until they got inside the car.

"Here, have some water," he said, passing him a bottle of Poland Springs. "It will help wash the bad taste out of your mouth."

· 3 ·

The Lay of the Land

Halfway to Harvard Square, Ed Masterson realized that he'd left his boat back at Riverside Boat Club, where the crime scene was still in progress. His mind was still flooded with images of Finley Sparks, floating in the water with his red splash jacket, like a giant Portuguese man-of-war. *No matter*, he thought; *he'd retrieve the boat tomorrow.* He was too cold and exhausted to row anymore.

As if sensing his passenger's state of shock, Lt. Rousseau drove along in silence, letting him warm up. "How about a coffee?" he finally asked, after a few minutes had passed.

Masterson nodded. He felt his body relax a bit, enveloped by the warmth of the squad car's generous heater. "So, what happened to the original Harvard Boathouse?" he said, recovering himself enough to make small talk.

"Weld?" Lt. Rousseau said. "It burned down, not long after it was built."

"Huh. I never knew that," Masterson admitted. "And I coached at Harvard for seven years." He gave a nervous laugh, and glanced over at Rousseau, who just smiled politely. The two men were roughly the same age, but there was something grounded about the lieutenant, which quickly put Masterson at ease.

"My father was a Boston cop," Rousseau volunteered, "so I grew up knowing the city beat when I joined patrol. Then I came to Harvard a few years ago, and my predecessor handed me a set of keys to all the Harvard buildings and encouraged me to learn where they all were located. It's quite a place for a history buff."

Masterson nodded, scanning the inside of the Ford Explorer. The center console had an array of modern tech, including an iPad held vertically by a detachable mount, and a police band radio sitting below it. Half of the backseat directly behind him was encased in hard plastic, where a suspect undoubtedly would go.

"Just out of curiosity, what happened to the old Crown Vics?" he asked.

"Oh, they went out a few years ago," Rousseau said, smiling again. "After that, we had the Ford Taurus for a few years. Neither one of them was great for inclement weather."

"You mean, like snow?" Masterson replied, pointing at the windshield. A few tiny flakes had begun to appear, bumping into the glass and bouncing off.

"Christ. It's not even Thanksgiving yet," Rousseau said, flicking on his wipers as he took a right off Memorial Drive onto JFK Street. After a few blocks, he took a quick left and parked in front of the Eliot Café, a glorified Dunkin' Donuts that sat right across from the Kennedy School of Government.

"Is this okay?" Rousseau asked. "Or are you a Starbucks man?"

"No, I like Dunkin'," Masterson admitted.

He scanned the café and spotted two seats, squeezed inside a pillar. The no-frills coffee shop was filled with an even mix of Harvard students and workmen. It was almost always full.

"Rough business, seeing a dead body for the first time," Rousseau said, joining Masterson at the table he'd found.

"Yeah. I've seen people at wakes, but this was different," Masterson admitted.

"Just out of curiosity, how well did you know the kid?"

"Pretty well," Masterson said. "I coached him for a while."

Rousseau took a sip of hot coffee and nodded.

"Finley never really did what he was told," Masterson elaborated. "He was a 'make-up-your-own-rules' type of guy, just like his father. Then again, a lot of Harvard kids can be that way."

"I know the father a little bit," Rousseau said. "He seems like a very successful, self-made man who donates a lot to different local organizations."

"Sheldon Sparks," Masterson scoffed. "Yes, a very generous guy to those he likes. He donated quite a bit to the Harvard crew program when his son was enrolled."

"Are you implying that he bought the kid's way in?"

Masterson shrugged. "Who knows? The old man rowed varsity crew for head coach Harry Parker, back in the heyday of Harvard rowing. Supposedly he was a pretty good oarsman. When I started coaching, Sheldon got really involved with the program for a while, in the annoying way some parents often do. He donated a few eight-oared shells, and then got himself onto the board of one of the big boatbuilding companies and practically took it over. Of course, he then wanted Harvard to buy all of his boats."

"Naturally. So, what was the kid like?"

"A real handful. Generally, I like coxswains to be a bit cocky, but Finley went too far. Even the guys in his own boat started to dislike him. And when I tried to rein him in, for his own sake, I found myself out of a job."

"Just because of that?"

Masterson paused. "Well, there was also the frostbite incident."

"Frostbite incident?" the lieutenant said. "What happened?"

"It was a cold day like today, with a bit of rain. Finley forgot his gloves, which he often did. Usually someone would lend him an extra pair, but that day no one did. I made him go out on the water anyway, partly to teach him a lesson."

Rousseau took a longer sip of coffee.

"Coxswains don't row, or even move much, so sitting still in the cold can be punishing. Long story short, Finley ended up getting frostbite. The family threatened to sue me and the college."

"How did that work out?"

"The Harvard attorneys eventually settled it out of court. I think part of the agreement was that I got let go from the college. Finley ended up losing a bit of his left pinky finger. I lost my job. He claimed that it ruined his ability to play the violin. Didn't stop him from making millions as a game developer, though."

"Well, now his musical career is definitely over, unless he plays the harp," Rousseau said.

Masterson looked down and tried not to smile.

"Sorry, bad joke," Rousseau said, laying his big hands flat on the table. "Look, if it's any consolation, nine times out of ten these things turn out to be suicides. Sometimes people jump right off the Mass Avenue Bridge."

"It's just so weird," Ed Masterson said. "I mean, I just saw him two days ago, coxing an alumni boat at the Head of the Charles. He seemed fine."

"Well, you heard the state police detective. It's no longer our concern. If the incident took place on the Harvard campus, it might be a different story. We're only here to assist if the big guys need help."

Rousseau glanced down at his Apple watch, then squinted as he checked his email on the tiny screen. "Sorry, I've got to run and cover my rounds. Do you need a lift back to your boat club or something?"

Masterson shook his head. "I can walk. It might help clear my head a bit."

The lieutenant rocked forward and rose out of his chair, laboring a bit to lift his heavy frame. Then he reached out and gave Masterson's hand another powerful squeeze and a reassuring pat on the shoulder. His broad smile was genuine and warm, and wrapped in his tan cardigan, he looked like someone's grandfather. Masterson felt marginally better.

"Do you really think he could have jumped?" he asked.

Rousseau tilted his head and winced.

"Well, based on what you've told me, a few things don't quite match up. First, the kid doesn't seem like the type. Second, the body was floating, only a day or so after he disappeared. That usually indicates that the lungs had air in them at the time of death."

"What does that mean?"

"It means that Finley Sparks was probably dead before he hit the water."

· 4 ·

The Living and the Dead

"*Well*, this is definitely not a case of death by immersion," Sue Chasen said, handing Delaney a pair of latex gloves as she escorted the detective into the autopsy room.

"How can you tell?" Delaney asked. He scanned the room before his eyes finally rested on the body of the deceased, laying unclothed on a metal gurney. This was one of the least favorite parts of his job, and Delaney was relieved that the lab wasn't full of other bodies in the process of disembowelment.

"Not enough water in the lungs. Of course, it could have been a 'dry drowning,'" she added. "A spasm in the airway."

Delaney nodded. "Anything else?"

"Well, there's a laceration on the back of the head, here," Chasen said, carefully repositioning Finley's head. Using a metal probe, she pointed to a sickle-shaped red gash about two-inches long, running along the back of his skull.

"Knife wound?" Delaney asked, looking first at Finley, then back at Chasen. He'd met the chief medical examiner only once before, and he wasn't sure how casually to interact with her yet, even though they were about the same age.

"I thought so at first, but it isn't clean enough. There's a fair amount of bruising around the wound as well, which suggests a blunt object."

"So, what is the cause of death?" Delaney asked.

It was the same question that Sheldon Sparks had demanded of him earlier that day when Delaney had accomplished the absolute least favorite part of his job—notifying the next of kin. Sheldon and his first wife, Irene, were due to arrive at the medical examiner's office that afternoon to officially ID their son, so Delaney wanted to have his story straight. Was it an accident, a suicide, or a homicide?

"I'll have to dig a bit deeper to establish that and try to determine if the wound was created after Mr. Sparks died and went into the river.

I'm also still waiting for the toxicology report," Chasen explained. "Until then, I can only speculate."

"Please do," Delaney said.

"Well, bloodshot eyes are usually a sure bet for asphyxiation. Plus, I did find some pulmonary granulosis," she said.

"Translation?"

"Inflammation in the lungs, usually due to particle inhalation."

"What kind of particles?"

Chasen shrugged. "Too soon to say."

Finley's face had turned a shade of whitish-green, and combined with his halo of red hair, he looked like a Halloween goblin. Delaney scanned the lab room again, seeking a distraction, but the sterile, stainless-steel sinks only reminded him of everything that happened here. He didn't know how anyone could handle this job, day after day.

"Do you think that cut could have been made with an oar?" Delaney asked, trying to return his focus to the laceration.

Chasen shook her head, and then grasped the detective's train of thought. "That might be too blunt an instrument to leave this sort of mark. Then again, a fin on the bottom of a boat could've done the job."

"Sounds like you know a lot about rowing," Delaney observed.

"Saint Paul's," Chasen said, grinning. "I sat bow seat in the girls' first boat."

"Impressive," Delaney said, smiling back.

"Well, it was several years ago," Chasen admitted. "Now the only exercise I get is lifting dead bodies around."

Delaney tried to suppress a laugh, which came out sounding like a sigh of relief.

"You look like a former athlete," she added.

"I played football at Matignon High."

"How barbaric," Chasen teased. "Speaking of head injuries and violence . . ."

"You mean, unlike rowing?" Delaney shot back, nodding toward Finley's corpse.

"You have a point there," Chasen said, looking down at the body and shaking her head. "I knew many oarsmen on the boys' team who suffered from some repressed feelings," she said, drawing a sheet over the body and lowering her voice, as if the corpse could hear.

"Translation, please?"

"Oarsmen like pain."

"Well, this guy was a coxswain, so I'm not sure that theory holds water, if you'll pardon the pun."

"*Au contraire*. It fits rather perfectly. Many coxswains like to inflict pain, so they are often resented by the oarsmen in the crew and tolerated as a necessary evil. A coxswain can verbally abuse the oarsmen while they are in the boat and the big guys simply have to sit there and take it."

"Reminds me of the DA," Delaney muttered. That morning, he'd outlined the details of the case with him over the phone, and then discussed whether there was enough suspicion to warrant a preliminary autopsy. During the talk, the high-strung attorney had berated him for not knowing who Sheldon Sparks was, then told him to move forward, despite the fact that the state had been making cutbacks.

"What about when they throw the guy into the water at the end of the race?" Delaney asked, still thinking about the DA.

"Oh, so you've heard about that?" Chasen said. "I'm impressed, detective. You've done your homework."

Delaney smiled, and then explained that he'd just spent the other part of his morning on the phone with Ted Harmsworth, the editor of gorow.com. In addition to a potential murder investigation, the detective had also been tasked with the more trivial duty of locating some stolen oars from the Head of the Charles Regatta.

"Stolen oars?" Chasen said, frowning. "Now that's unusual."

"You mean, unlike finding a dead body floating in the river?" Delaney said.

"*Touché*, detective."

"I'm sorry," Delaney said, finally expressing his frustration. "I mean, maybe I'm just a simple football player, but rowing seems like a weird sport, filled with privileged people with a lot of hang-ups."

Chasen clucked her tongue then glowered at him in a playful way.

"Well, now that we've both let our hair down, so to speak, there are two more things I need to show you which may lend some validity to that opinion," Chasen said, lifting up the sheet again.

"There's an interesting little owl tattoo on his forearm," she said, flipping it palm side up. "And you should be familiar with these marks," she added, flipping the body over, pointing further down, at Finley's wrists.

"Handcuffs?"

The chief medical examiner raised her eyebrows and gave the inspector a bemused look.

"But if there was no bruising around the head wound, how can there be bruising here?"

"Different time frame. These marks obviously happened prior to the cause of death, whatever that was."

Delaney shook his head, and then studied the owl tattoo. It was resting within an equilateral triangle, set with three small Greek letters emblazoned within the vertices. If the victim weren't so well off, he would have considered it as a possible mark of gang membership.

"Bizarre. Can you tell me the time of death at least?"

"It's difficult with cold water, of course, but I'd guess around midnight to 2 a.m. last night."

Delaney stood looking at Finley Sparks in silence for a long moment. The last time he'd seen a dead body up close was at his mother's wake, a year ago. Open caskets were a gruesome affair, but his father had insisted on it.

"What are you thinking?" the coroner asked, snapping him out of his reverie.

"Oh sorry," Delaney said. "Honestly, I don't know what to say about this one."

Chasen nodded in agreement.

"Drowning can be tricky, but the toxicology report should help clear some things up."

Another few moments passed, as they both continued to look over the corpse.

"Pretty short life," Delaney mused, shaking his head.

"Yeah. But maybe an interesting one."

"Is that a professional opinion," Delaney said, giving his colleague a half-smile, "or are you speaking for the dead now?"

"Well, if we don't speak for them, who will?" Chasen asked.

· 5 ·

No Good Deed

$\mathcal{E}$d Masterson made his way back to his truck, walking along the Cambridge side of the Charles River beneath a canopy of giant sycamores. When Masterson walked, it sometimes looked like he was carrying a 75-pound pack on his back, leaning forward with heavy footfalls set with great deliberation, as if he were climbing a mountain. Today, he looked particularly fatigued, overburdened with the events of the morning. On his left he could see Newell, the Harvard men's boathouse, and on his right was the gray stone monastery of St. John the Evangelist.

He laughed to himself as he remembered how his old boss, Harry Parker, used to tee up golf balls on the Newell dock and drive them across the river, aiming for the flock of Canadian geese that often rested on the grassy bank in great numbers. Parker hated the geese with such a passion that out on the river, coaching his crews, he would sometimes direct the coxswains to aim straight for them, hoping that the oarsmen might take out a few as they rowed hard and fast. Masterson often wondered how much that sadistic streak had allowed Parker and his crews to win so many races.

The Charles was almost perfectly calm now, devoid of boats, and Masterson gazed at it the way some people studied a piece of art. To him, the river possessed a constant, mysterious beauty, with colors and shapes and textures that all kept shifting like a giant, unsolvable puzzle, or an impressionist painting that changed depending on your position to it. After the passing snowfall, the sun had come out and spread across the surface of the water, turning it into a silvery, liquid mirror, and the cold gave the water a heavier quality, like mercury.

Out in the middle of the river, there were patches of colored light that broke into a thousand tiny pieces where the wind brushed it, and each of them caught a different shade of the blues and grays of the November sky, and occasionally the dark outline of a passing cloud. Along the far bank, it was inky black and completely opaque, but closer in, under the shadow of the sycamores, he could gaze straight through it and see the bottom. The brown water was only partly clear and looked like it was flecked with old coffee grounds.

There were rare moments when he would be out on the Charles, just sitting in his boat at the end of a hard workout and enjoying the brief sensation of tranquility. It was a good feeling, even though it didn't last long. Now, even that was gone, replaced by the memory of Finley's body floating face down in the water. When the frogmen had rolled him over, exposing his face, some part of Masterson had seized up and been held captive. Now it was like a bad dream that kept recurring, leaving him in a less certain state of mind. It was a familiar, unpleasant sensation that he'd felt before, almost a year ago to the day.

* * * * *

He'd been derigging a boat in the boathouse bays, getting ready to put it away for winter storage, when he suddenly heard screeching tires, followed by a *thunk* and then a loud splash. When he slid open the big bay doors out to the river, he saw a commercial van, sinking nose down into the river.

For a moment he just stood there, trying to figure out how something so large could have possibly gotten so far out into the river. The van looked completely out of place there, floating in the water, like one of those Boston Harbor duck boats that hauled truckloads of tourists around every summer. While he was debating what to do, two state police cruisers arrived with their sirens blasting, and two officers with life vests and a towrope jumped into the water without hesitation. *Dumb move*, he thought. The water was freezing.

Masterson grabbed his single scull and quickly launched from the Harvard dock, paddling steadily. By now the two policemen had managed to open the back doors of the van and pulled out the driver, who'd suffered a temporary seizure but was now fully conscious. Remarkably, the guy was completely fine but in a total state of panic. Cold water could do that to you, not to mention flying off the highway at 60 miles per hour and catapulting into the Charles River. As Masterson drew near, he also noticed that the two cops were getting hypothermia from the frigid water, and they clearly had no good rescue plan except the rope.

"Have him hold onto the front of my boat," Masterson suggested. The cops reluctantly went along with the plan, knowing that they would soon become useless.

Clinging to the bow, the panicked man immediately started screaming at Masterson to row harder. Luckily, the long bow of the shell kept some distance between him and the crazy van driver, who scrambled to shore as soon as his legs touched bottom and ran away without uttering a word of thanks. Masterson hung out for a while, idling in his boat, and then left when the police no longer seemed to need him. He, too, was starting to get cold. As he rowed away, he saw the caravan of local news trucks and a WBZ helicopter arrive on the scene, eager to get a story for the evening news.

Two hours later, Masterson was shopping for Christmas presents at Best Buy in Watertown. Staring at a bank of new TV sets, he watched a newscaster cover the event, referring to him as "an unidentified man in a rowboat" who risked his own safety in the rescue effort. Without warning, his whole body started shaking uncontrollably, a delayed reaction to the danger he'd put himself in, combined with the fact that no one had ever thanked him afterward.

* * * * *

Now, as Masterson walked along the Charles, he felt an echo of that uninvited sense of panic creep back into his veins. Convincing himself that it was merely the cold, he jumped into his truck at Cambridge Boat Club and got the engine and the heater going full blast. Then he headed down to Riverside to pick up his boat. He'd left it outside, without a cover, and there was no fence or gate around the public rowing facility to protect it from curious passersby. He hoped that the crowd and the law enforcement vehicles that had gathered there this morning had dispersed by now and he could sneak in and out without attracting any attention. It was an expensive boat, after all, and he didn't want anyone or anything messing with it.

When he pulled into the Riverside parking lot, he spotted two state police officers lifting his boat off the outside storage rack and clumsily trying to transfer it onto a nearby cargo van. A woman in a white jumpsuit was hovering nearby, along with the state police detective he'd spoken with earlier this morning. The woman was holding a plastic baggie in her gloved hands, and the patrol officers were manhandling the delicate shell. They obviously had no idea of how to carry it properly. A makeshift tarp had been suspended over the rack where he'd left the boat, using a sheet of heavy plastic.

"Hey!" he yelled, jumping out of his truck. "Be careful with that. It's my boat!"

"We know," Sean Delaney said, intercepting him. "That's why we're impounding it." His voice was flat, and his expression lacked the warmth that had been there that morning.

"Why? I mean, what the hell is going on?"

"Quite possibly a murder investigation," Delaney said. "We're treating this as a suspicious death now." He looked directly at Masterson as he said this, waiting to see what his reaction would be. Masterson stopped in his tracks and looked like he'd just been gut punched.

"What? Why?"

"I thought you told me you didn't touch the body," Delaney asked.

"I didn't," Masterson said.

"Well, we think your boat may have, so we want to test it for traces of DNA; particularly that little black rudder on the bottom of it."

"You mean the fin?" Masterson asked, indignantly.

"Whatever you want to call it," Delaney said.

"Well, maybe my boat did bump into the body—so what? I mean, Finley must've already been dead," Masterson parried.

The inspector looked at him for a moment, enjoying the growing uncertainty in Masterson's voice. He had to admit, part of him liked playing the interrogation game.

"We don't know that for sure," Delaney pointed out.

"But it doesn't make any sense!" Masterson objected.

Delaney shrugged. "I'm afraid you'll need to come down to the state police barracks and give us another statement. And this time, tell us everything."

"But I'm the one who found the body," Masterson protested. "And now you are treating me like some sort of suspect?"

"Relax, sir. I never said that," Delaney said, softening his tone. "We just need a few more details. It's a routine part of an investigation," he added.

They both looked over to see the two patrol officers, who had now laid the wooden shell upside down on the hard ground, resting on its riggers. They were encasing it in the plastic that had been used to create the examination tent. One of them looked vaguely familiar to Masterson, but he couldn't quite place him.

"At least let me show your guys how to handle my boat so they don't damage it," Masterson said. "It's worth a lot of money."

"That's fine, just don't touch it," Delaney said. He called over to the patrol officers, giving Masterson permission to assist in the loading process.

The two cops had little idea about what to do with the 25-foot-long racing shell, and even less concern about the boat's value. Masterson fetched some tie-down straps and wrenches from his truck and took over, directing them as to how to derig the boat and place it properly onto the van's primitive roof rack. After the single was correctly positioned and secured, he got them to tie a red signal flag on the stern to indicate overhang. Then Masterson got in the van with them and headed off toward the state police barracks, while Delaney followed in his squad car.

On the way, the two officers tried to make small talk with Masterson, reassuring him that everything would be fine. The guy driving explained that he knew a little bit about boats, since his dad owned an old rust bucket that they both went fishing in, out on Boston Harbor. The outboard was worth less than the Charlestown mooring it sat on, he explained, but during the summer his father spent more time on it than he spent at home, sometimes just listening to Red Sox games on an old portable radio while he polished off a six pack of Narragansett Ale.

Masterson just listened and didn't reply. The man was trying to be nice, but he was clearly ignorant about rowing. As they crossed over the Charles River and onto Soldier's Field Road, Masterson looked out the window and suddenly remembered where he'd seen him before; he'd been one of the two police officers who tried to rescue the van driver who'd nearly drowned in the Charles River, only a year ago.

Masterson laughed to himself at the circularity of things. In both cases, he'd done something that he thought was right, but there was nothing and no one to confirm his good intentions or to erase the voodoo of sheer panic that had been transferred to him from the drowning victim. And now, to add insult to injury, he was going to lose his prized King single for a while. The same boat that had once rescued a man out on the Charles River was now being treated as a possible murder weapon.

• 6 •

The Sins of the Father

Sheldon Sparks had the look of a man who had feasted on all the pleasures of life and was now suffering from a bad case of indigestion.

In the 30 years since he'd graduated from the Harvard Business School, he'd accumulated a multimillion-dollar fortune composed of various speculative investments, mostly in real estate and the high-tech industry. He'd also been married three times, had six children, and added about 80 extra pounds of girth to his formerly athletic frame. The extra heft was distributed about his midsection like the ballast on a hot air balloon, but he didn't seem embarrassed by it. Instead, as he strode down the main corridor of 1 Bullfinch Place, he bestowed a patriarchal nod or a smile to anyone who noticed his plus-sized presence, elegantly clad in a Brooks Brothers suit.

Making a beeline toward assistant DA Tim Prendergast's office, he wheeled to his left and then to his right, pivoting his entire upper body like the turret of a tank in order to shamelessly peer into other people's offices. When he wasn't smiling a fake smile, his large, fleshy face had the pugnacious expression of a bulldog, and his eyes bore the wrinkles and dark rings of a career insomniac.

"Well, have you caught the bastard who killed my son yet?" he blurted out, stepping into the ADA's room. Despite the overall depravity of his character, his energy and intellect were both quite intact, and they came out in rapid-fire bursts.

"Sheldon, please, have a seat. I think you've already met Inspector Delaney?"

"Yeah, we met in the coroner's office," he said. "So, what've you got?"

Delaney hesitated for a second, glancing over at Tim Prendergast. The ADA gave him a curt nod. Normally, neither one of them was at liberty to disclose information about an ongoing case, even to a family member of the deceased.

"Well, we are questioning a few people, including the former Harvard crew coach who found your son's body," Delaney said, trying to be as vague as possible. He'd just left the Ed Masterson interview in the hands of his second-in-command when he'd gotten the urgent call from Tim Prendergast, and he wasn't very happy about it.

"Yeah. That's the guy. He did it."

"Now Sheldon . . ." Prendergast started.

"I want you to lock him up and throw away the key," Sparks continued. He leaned over and whispered coarsely to Delaney: "Stick a fork in him, if you know what I mean."

Delaney raised his eyebrows and glanced over at his colleague for help.

"Do whatever you need to do. Money is no object here," Sparks added.

"Sheldon, please," Prendergast finally cut in. "You know things don't work that way."

"Sure, they do. Everything does." He looked back and forth between Prendergast and Delaney like an innocent child who'd just eaten a big slice of chocolate cake before dinner and couldn't understand what was wrong.

"I should tell you that we have a new DA who is, well, a woman. She's the first female DA we've ever had in Boston, and she is very much opposed to unnecessary incarceration."

"Who?"

"Her name is Rhonda Rodriguez."

"Sounds like an exotic dancer I used to date," Sparks said, in a raspy baritone. "What is she, some sort of minority hire?" He glanced over at Delaney to gauge his reaction to the crude remarks.

Tim Prendergast shook his head, while Delaney remained silent. Some of the guys back at the State Police barracks still talked like this, but less and less so as the composition and age of the force changed with the times, along with a growing awareness about sexual harassment and diversity.

"She's actually smart as a whip and well respected," Prendergast said. "And she doesn't like spending resources on anything but the most serious cases."

"What the hell does that mean, Tim? You think this isn't serious? Christ, my son just got killed and dumped into the Charles River! It's like the Winter Hill gang all over again."

"Sir, with all due respect," Delaney said, "we don't know exactly what happened yet." Sparks glared at him and then turned back toward the ADA.

"Who is this guy, your second string?"

"Sheldon, please. Inspector Delaney is a very capable officer."

"I don't want capable; I want a pit bull. Whatever happened to Bob Rousseau?"

"He's the chief of police at Harvard now," Prendergast said.

"Smart man. How about we bring him in as a consultant?"

Prendergast shook his head.

"What's the big deal?" Sparks said. "Let him team up with green-horn here. After all, two heads are better than one."

"With all due respect sir, I work alone," Delaney said.

"Nobody works alone. You get nowhere alone. Trust me, kid, I've tried it."

Prendergast tried to wipe the stress off his face with his hands, then leaned back in his chair and glanced over at his colleague. The young inspector appeared to be calm and confident. In reality, Delaney was desperately trying to resist the urge to reach over and slap the arrogant multimillionaire across the face, just to see what he would do. People reacted differently to the death of a family member, but he'd never seen this sort of outrageous behavior before. Who cared if he had deep contacts in city government and local real estate?

Just then, Delaney felt his cellphone buzz in his pocket. "Toxicology just texted. I should go check it out," he said quietly.

"Saved by the bell," Sheldon Sparks quipped.

"Sorry for your loss, Mr. Sparks. I'll be in touch."

"Yeah, sure. Just find out how he died. And if there was any foul play, I'll take care of it myself."

* * * * *

Leaving the ADA's office, Delaney wondered if Sheldon Sparks would make good on such a threat. He doubted it. Still, he made sure that he was well clear of listening range before ringing up the coroner's office.

"And I thought you'd never call," Sue Chasen teased him.

"Trust me, I've been dying to get back to you," Delaney replied.

"C'mon now, is that the best you can do?" Chasen said. He had to admit, it was nice to hear the lighthearted and intelligent tone of Sue's voice after listening to the ravings of a self-important boor.

"Okay, St. Paul's. What've you got?" he said.

"Well, you may not like this, but we found traces of Fentanyl in Finley's blood samples."

"Fentanyl, as in the opiate?"

"Yep."

"Well, that changes things a bit."

"I'd say so."

"So, if it was a drug overdose, that might explain the likelihood of death prior to drowning?"

"It might," Chasen said, noncommittal with her tone of voice. "We also found something else that was a little curious—oil samples on the clothes."

"What kind of oil?"

"We're working on that now, but it looks like two stroke motor oil."

"Like the kind you put into an outboard engine?"

"Or a lawnmower," Chasen baited.

"Yeah, but how many people are mowing their lawns in November?"

"Oh, very good, detective. You get a gold star!"

"And a beer after work?" he ventured.

"Absolutely not," she said. "Just looking at beer makes my stomach queasy."

"Sorry to hear that," he apologized.

"Yes, I'm afraid you'll have to drink whiskey if you're drinking with me. I'll text you an address and a time later."

Chasen abruptly hung up, as Delaney hopped into his squad car to head back to barracks. He felt like he could use that whiskey now, after dealing with Sheldon Sparks, but the rest of the day still lay ahead of him, including the equally difficult task of cross-examining Edward Masterson. But at least this time, he'd be asking the hard questions.

• 7 •

Good Cop, Bad Cop

*W*hen Sean Delaney had told Sheldon that he worked alone, he wasn't telling the literal truth. The Massachusetts State Police employed the same basic protocol and hierarchy as any police or military force did, which meant that Delaney had a sergeant and a lieutenant above him, overseeing his work, and at least a few patrol officers below, assisting in different ways. By now, everyone had at least heard something about the Charles River drowning. And while Delaney had been designated as the primary investigator on the Sparks case, he also had been teamed up with a second officer named Marshall McDonald, affectionately known around the barracks as "Marsh."

Having a second officer came in handy, especially when you were pulled in two different directions at the same time or needed to multitask as they had this morning when Delaney had been called over to the DA's office. Marsh was super reliable and had a great memory for details, but he was young and lacked focus. He also lacked the ability to put himself inside a criminal's mind or even read social cues while interviewing a witness. Either because of this, or as a way to compensate, he relied heavily on technology. He was constantly fiddling with his cellphone and spouting useless facts that he gleaned from Google.

"Hey, Delaney, do you know that a cow has four stomachs?" Marsh said, as the sergeant entered the old brick barracks and found his partner idling in front of the interview room, along with IT specialist, Anthony DeFavio.

"Marsh, what's going on here?" Delaney said, ignoring the remark. "How come the door to the interview room is shut? This is supposed to be a friendly interview, correct?"

Marsh barely diverted his eyes from his phone and then blinked, revealing a mild case of nearsightedness. He gave a forced, appeasing smile.

"Relax, Sean. There's no problem here," DeFavio intervened. I got Masterson a cup of coffee and gave him a tour of the barracks. Then the three of us had a nice little chat about rowing while we were waiting for you."

"It's so cool that he's a crew coach, don't you think?" Marsh added.

Delaney stared at his partner and bit his tongue.

"Did you find out anything important?"

"Well, I did dig up a few interesting bits and pieces online, like a lawsuit by the victim's family against Masterson when he was a Harvard coach a few years ago . . . something about frostbite. I just sent you the link to the *Boston Globe* article."

Delaney pulled out his phone and quickly skimmed the article. Then he entered the interview room, leaving the door wide open. Marsh followed him in.

Certain protocols had to be observed if a witness wasn't there to be interrogated. Primarily, they had to feel like they could come and go as they pleased and provide information freely without the fear that it might be used against them. It was all a matter of tone. If the questions got too pointed, a witness might clam up, but then again, some people were naturally shy and needed to be prodded. Once they started talking, however, things could change. Occasionally, during an interview, someone might inadvertently say something incriminating, or simply false, and then you had to put them under caution and read them their rights. That's when they went from being a witness to a suspect.

"Sorry to have kept you waiting," Delaney said to Ed Masterson, and shook his hand. "I hope my colleague here has treated you well?"

"Well enough," Masterson said, glancing over at Marsh.

"So, I was just speaking with the father of the deceased," Delaney said. "Sheldon Sparks?"

Masterson shook his head. "Don't believe anything that guy tells you."

The inspector chuckled good-naturedly.

"So how would you describe your relationship to his son when you were his coach?"

Masterson shifted in his seat. "Mostly normal."

"What about the frostbite incident?" Marsh blurted out. Delaney shot him a quick sideways glance.

Masterson shook his head. "Like I told the Harvard cop, Finley forgot to wear gloves. It was a cold day. I don't know what more there is to say."

"Bob Rousseau?" Delaney asked. "When did you speak to him?"

"We had coffee the day I reported the drowning."

Delaney tried to suppress a frown.

"Okay, but from now on, please don't discuss the case with anyone."

"Fine by me," Masterson said.

"So, it sounds like you and Finley's father didn't get along?" Delaney continued, trying to steer the conversation back onto easier ground.

Masterson laughed. "Oh, we got along all right. He even invited my fiancée and me over to his house for a barbeque, along with the rest of the Harvard coaching staff and a few former Olympians."

"When was that?" He looked over at Marsh, who was now busy taking notes like he was supposed to.

"A few years ago, when I was still working at Harvard."

"So, what changed? The guy doesn't seem to like you very much now," Delaney joked.

"Where should I begin?" Masterson scoffed. "First of all, at the barbeque, he took me out to his 'auto barn' and showed me his sports car collection, which included a Ferrari, a Maserati, a Jaguar E type, and an Aston Martin DB5."

"The James Bond Car," Marsh stated, matter-of-factly. Delaney gave him another quick look of mild annoyance, but Masterson simply nodded.

"'This is the car that 007 drove in *Dr. No*,' he told me. 'I'll sell it to you for 3 million. Or you can just let me sleep with your fiancée.' Then he laughed, one of those big laughs that tries to make everyone else in the room feel small."

"And what did you say?"

Masterson gave the inspector a sour look.

"I told him I liked my pickup truck just fine."

Delaney chuckled again.

"Then he asked me to buy a bunch of crew shells for the program from a boat company he'd just joined as a board member. I said 'no' to that request, too, but later the head coach overruled me."

"What was his reaction?"

"Not many people say 'no' to Sheldon Sparks."

"Yeah, I got that same impression," Delaney muttered, looking over his case notes. Out of his peripheral vision he noticed that Marsh was back on his cellphone, multitasking while taking notes.

"So, do you think your relationship with Finley's father might have influenced the way you treated Finley himself?" Delaney asked.

"I don't think so. But I certainly didn't want to give any special attention to the kid, just because he was a legacy."

"And did he have any enemies that you knew of?"

"I'm pretty sure most of his teammates hated him," Masterson said.

"Why do you say that? Did the team do poorly?"

"Quite the reverse. The final year I coached them, they went undefeated."

"So how come the lack of brotherly love?" Delaney asked.

"Finley was a nasty little guy, sarcastic as hell. Often, he'd try to get the guys to row harder by taunting them with personal insults."

"Like what?"

Masterson shrugged. "'You guys row like old people have sex—slow and sloppy.' Comments like that."

Marsh laughed.

"Is that all?" Delaney pressed.

"Look, I can't remember many specifics, but some of it was pretty bad stuff. He'd ferret out who had failed a class, or who had just broken up with a girlfriend, and he'd then broadcast that information over the speaker system of the boat, often during the middle of a race."

"But wouldn't that sort of thing create dissent?"

"In the long run, maybe. In the short run, well, they were national champions. So go figure. Some people are motivated by abuse."

Delaney nodded, thinking back to a drill sergeant he had at the academy who had pushed the recruits beyond their limits, but everyone understood that the occasional rough behavior was only meant to toughen them up.

Somehow, what Finley had done seemed different, even vindictive.

"And I thought rowing was all about teamwork," Marsh said, reemerging from his internet fugue. This time both Masterson and Delaney looked at him, frowning.

"You have to understand," Masterson continued. "Almost every Harvard kid is an overachiever. If you tell them terrible things about themselves, they often just try harder to overcompensate. Finley understood this, and he used verbal abuse as a motivational tool."

"Or more like a weapon," Delaney said. "But why did they tolerate that sort of thing? By the sound of it, he seemed like a real jerk."

"Good coxswains are hard to find," Masterson explained. "Finley had excellent basic skills, like steering. Plus, his boat won races, and in the end that's all that matters to serious athletes."

"I get that," Delaney said, then cocked his head to one side, looking over his notes. "But are you sure there wasn't anything else involved?"

"Well, I sometimes sensed that some of the guys on the team were a little afraid of Finley, or of what he might find out and use against them. Rumor had it that he got most of his personal information by hacking into the student files from the Harvard intranet. Apparently, he was a computer prodigy, which is unsurprising given his father's position at Oracle."

"Kind of a chip off the old block?" Delaney said.

"Exactly."

"So, when was the last time you saw him?"

"Last weekend, actually. I saw him out on the river, coxing a crew. He must have been training for an alumni race in the Head of the Charles. I hollered to the boat, but Finley didn't wave back. I don't think he ever forgave me for the frostbite."

Delaney nodded. "So, you have no idea who might want to hurt him?"

"Hurt him, yes. Kill him, no."

"Who?"

"Anyone in that boat. Seriously. The only time they could ever get back at him was when they got to throw him into the river after they'd won a race. Are you familiar with the tradition?"

"I'm not," Marsh said.

"It's a post-race victory thing, where the oarsmen of the winning crew grab their coxswain and toss him into the water. Usually, it's pretty benign, but these guys would often throw Finley extra high, hoping he'd land painfully or belly flop."

"Well, it looks like he got thrown into the river for the last time," Marsh said, with a blank-faced expression.

Masterson and Delaney both looked at him, and then exchanged a look.

"Okay, I think we've troubled you quite enough for one day," Delaney said. "One last thing, though. Do you still have a list of Finley's former teammates?"

"Sure, I can write it down for you," Masterson said. "Most of the guys have graduated by now, but I imagine that you can get their contact information from the alumni office."

Delaney nodded. "Do you have any questions for us?"

"Yeah. When can I get my boat back?" Masterson asked.

"Probably soon," Delaney said. "They should be done testing it for evidence. In the meanwhile, I'll have one of the patrol officers give you a lift back to the river."

"Thanks," Masterson said, glumly, and started to make his way out to the front exit.

Delaney turned toward Marsh and shook his head, trying to find the right words to say to his young colleague about his performance during the interview.

"Well, I don't think he had anything to do with it," Marsh said, interjecting before Delaney could express his disapproval.

"And why do you say that?" Delaney played along, pinching his lower lip.

"Well, if he was lying, he would have laughed at my jokes. I mean, nobody who is innocent ever laughs at my jokes."

Delaney felt his anger suddenly give way to surprise, and then unexpected levity.

"Marsh, that's a completely random and yet somehow valid observation," he laughed. "Still, you're going to have to get better at this interview game."

Marsh nodded, eager for approval from his senior colleague. "I'll go make sure that Masterson has a ride," he said and quickly left the room.

Delaney shook his head and then checked his phone. A text had come through from Sue Chasen at the coroner's office. "The Seven's Bar, Beacon Hill 8 p.m."

And now he was really looking forward to that whiskey. He could already taste it on his lips.

· 8 ·

Collaboration

On his way out of the barracks, Delaney poked his head inside Joe Martinoli's office. Martinoli was sitting down at his desk, finishing up a phone call as he looked out his window at the Museum of Science. He motioned the inspector to come in and have a seat, while he spit out the final pieces of a conversation that he clearly didn't want to be having.

"Yes. No. Of course. Got it. Understood. You, too. Bye."

Even a few years past his retirement age, Martinoli was still a devoted workaholic who showed no signs of slowing down, despite a recent and messy divorce, a triple bypass surgery, and a fierce nicotine habit that he was unsuccessfully trying to control with an arm patch.

"Okay, I don't know how you swung it, Sean, but I just got off the phone with the DA's office, and your investigation is now officially a 'go.'"

Delaney smiled. He liked the chief, despite the fact that he was rough around the edges and openly abusive to everyone, including himself.

"Damn this patch," he said, tearing it off his arm. "Doesn't work for shit. Where the hell is my nicotine gum?" He rifled through his desk drawer until he located his stash, then popped a piece into his mouth and started chewing furiously.

"So, what have you got? Tell me some good news," Martinoli said.

"One witness, with not much to share; an angry parent of the deceased, wanting revenge; and some new information from the coroner, who may have just found some traces of Fentanyl in the victim's blood. I'm going to see her now."

Martinoli chewed and nodded, folding his hands together on top of his desk. "So, what's your game plan?"

"I'd like to have a couple of patrol officers canvass the boathouses along the Charles River to try to find out if anyone else saw something last weekend."

"During the Head of the Charles?" Martinoli scoffed. "That's a needle in a haystack. Don't more people attend that event than the Boston marathon?"

"Maybe," Delaney admitted. "But it takes place in a more contained area. And I'd like to know exactly where that body went in the water."

"Okay, fine. What about tech?"

"The victim's cellphone was submerged for quite a while, but we should be able to pull some data from it. We've yet to search his room, which could be tricky until the father calms down a bit."

"The kid lived at home?"

"Apparently."

Martinoli shook his head. "Typical millennial. Meanwhile, my kids won't even come and visit me anymore. They always run to their mother."

Delaney said nothing, just smiled politely when his boss looked at him.

"Well, get on it. Track down every call and email you can find."

"Will do."

"And be careful with that coroner, Sue Chasen. Rumor has it that she eats boys for breakfast."

Delaney laughed. "Thanks, chief. I think I can take care of myself."

"That's what they all say," Martinoli jeered. "Then you find yourself working past retirement age, sitting behind a desk and chewing nicotine gum."

"Duly noted, boss. I'll be careful out there."

* * * * *

The Sevens Ale House was one of those classic Irish bars that somehow still existed on Charles Street, tucked inconspicuously between high-end antique shops and gourmet food stores. It was the perfect hideaway for someone who wanted to sit quietly and sip a decent beer or catch a Celtics game on the big screen TV without getting bothered by a nosy tourist.

Sue Chasen was already waiting for Delaney, seated at the bar in a ladder-backed chair nursing a vodka martini. Out of her scrubs, wearing a cashmere sweater and designer jeans, she looked classy and attractive. For a second, he just stopped and stared, adjusting the prior image he had stored in his brain of her.

"Well, what took you so long? Did you get lost?" she said, finishing up a text. Then she looked up and smiled, showing off her perfect white teeth.

"Yeah, I think I took a wrong turn and ended up at Alibi."

"You mean that fancy bar at the Liberty Hotel?"

"Yeah. That's the one."

"I guess we could've gone there," Chasen said. "I just figured it was a little too close to home for you, being an old prison and all only a few years ago."

"I remember it well," Delaney said, smiling. "Some of my acquaintances from high school ended up there as inmates."

"Nice friends!"

"I said 'acquaintances,' not friends," he corrected.

"You did, indeed," Chasen said. "And just out of curiosity, which of those two am I?"

"That depends," he said. "What've you got for me?"

"Straight to business. I like your style."

Delaney shrugged. "What can I say? I'm a cop."

"Another vodka martini for me," Chasen said to the bartender, "And for my acquaintance—"

"Club soda," Delaney said.

"Really? How boring, I thought you said you liked beer?"

"Yes, but I'm officially still on duty for another ten minutes. You look nice, by the way."

Chasen reached down and pulled a folder out of her backpack, shaking her head at Delaney's clumsy attempt at flattery. Her brown hair briefly spilled around her shoulders, reminding him of a girl he had dated in high school.

"Here's the toxicology report," she said. "There was enough Fentanyl in his system to take down an elephant. Make that two elephants."

"So, the question is *why*? I mean, was Finley Sparks actually a user, or did he just go to a party and get in over his head?"

"Well, he didn't have needle marks on his body, just that stupid tattoo, so I suspect it was the latter scenario. He must have ingested it in powder form, snorted like cocaine. Sadly, most people who play around with opioids don't know what they are getting themselves into, though, especially if it's purchased on the street."

"How come?"

"Fentanyl is often mixed together with other things, like benzos and crushed opioid pills, and then the unstable mixture is sold as heroin."

"Is that what they call 'scramble' heroin?" Delaney asked.

Chasen nodded. "It scrambles your brain, alright. Fentanyl is 50 to 100 times more powerful than morphine. It doesn't take much to take you down."

"That's probably why they are starting to require us to use certain precautions when approaching anyone who might have been in contact with the drug, like wearing face masks and gloves. Apparently even a slight amount of the powder form can knock a guy flat."

"Well, we certainly wouldn't want that," Chasen smiled, sipping her vodka. "I guess you're damn lucky that this kid was found in water rather than on dry land."

"I'll drink to that," Delaney said, raising his glass of club soda.

Chasen frowned, keeping her glass on the bar. "Are ten minutes up yet? Can you have a beer and relax a bit?"

"No, but I'll have a shot of Jameson's."

"Wow. Switching to hardcore now. I like that."

"Well, I have to catch up to your two vodka martinis."

Overhearing the last bit of their conversation, the elderly bartender poured out the whiskey and set it down on the countertop in front of Delaney. The two men acknowledged one another, and then Delaney glanced up at the TV above the bar, where the six o'clock news was playing and something that caught his eye. A female reporter was standing by the banks of the Charles, underdressed for the weather in a fancy trench coat.

"No leads have yet been disclosed about the mysterious drowning of an ex-Harvard student, Finley Sparks, who was found washed up near the Boston University Bridge only three days ago," she announced. Photos of Finley Sparks flashed across the screen, no doubt gathered from the internet, and then the reporter played a prerecorded interview with his illustrious father, Sheldon Sparks, who was described as a stalwart in the business community.

"I hope they get on this right away and bring the responsible parties to justice," Sparks said in a gravelly voice, staring directly into the camera.

"Damn," Delaney said. "He should know better than to talk to the press like that. Now they'll be crawling all over me."

"He seems like a loose cannon," Chasen said.

"Totally. He's getting on my nerves."

"Have another shot of whiskey?"

"I'm good," Delaney said. "I wouldn't mind getting some fresh air, though, if you don't mind."

"Sure thing. Maybe you can walk me back to my place, just up the Hill."

"You mean Beacon Hill?" he said, grinning. "How does a city coroner manage to rub shoulders with the Brahmins, if you don't mind me asking?"

"Maybe because I was married to one of them," she said, bluntly.

"Wow, you are full of surprises," he said.

"But not full of money," she quipped. "So, you can pay the bill to make up for your impertinence."

Delaney laughed and started to pull some cash out of his wallet. The elderly bartender waved his money aside.

"Interesting. Is that one of your acquaintances, too?" Sue Chasen asked.

"Sure," he said. "That's my old high school math teacher, Mr. O'Reilly."

"Very funny. You're joking, right?"

"What do you think?" Delaney said, smiling.

"I think you're a bit more complex than I thought."

It had been a while since Delaney had navigated his way through the warren of narrow streets that constituted Beacon Hill, the historic spit of land on top of which sat the golden domed State House. The social demographic there was a bit out of his league, and he didn't care to gawk at the elegant, federal-style brick row houses, many of which looked like something out of a Charles Dickens novel. Out of their doors emerged the Boston elites; bankers, politicians, and lawyers, men and women who dressed in full-length, camel-hair coats and suits tailored at Brooks Brothers. Men like Sheldon Sparks.

"I still can't believe that idiot went to the news media," Delaney lamented.

"Maybe they came to him," Chasen said. "And you know a guy like that can't keep his mouth shut."

"You're probably right."

"Forget about it," Chasen said, taking him by the arm. "Look, the Christmas decorations are already up. Pretty magical, don't you think?"

"Yeah, I suppose," he admitted.

"What a romantic," she said, as they slowed down to a full stop in front of her apartment building.

"Well?" she said, looking at her watch.

"Well, what?" Delaney replied.

"Is it time to make out now?" Sue Chasen asked, smiling brightly.

"Excuse me?" Delaney said, choking down a laugh.

"Well, I don't know about you, but I have to wake up early tomorrow, so if you're going to put the moves on me, let's fast forward this a bit."

"Talk about romantic!" he laughed.

"What can I say?" Chasen smiled. "I'm a coroner. The way I see it, life is short."

"Amen to that," he said, following her inside.

· 9 ·

The Sign of the Owl

$\mathcal{D}$elaney was in a half-awake state of consciousness about an hour or so before dawn. He dreamed he was walking through a grove of old cedar trees. As he walked, his feet sank into the mossy earth. Everything was silent. Suddenly he realized that he had entered an ancient cemetery. Something, or someone, was watching him. He paused briefly to have a look around. He heard the noise first, and then he spotted it. Perched in the branches of a cedar tree was a pair of shining amber eyes. An owl. It started hooting, as if sounding an alarm.

He woke to the sound of his cellphone, buzzing on vibrate. A text appeared when the call went unanswered.

"Damn," he said softly, reading it.

Sue Chasen lay beside him, breathing softly with her mouth slightly open. It looked like she was still asleep. Delaney got up, slid on his trousers and shirt, and quietly tried to make his way out the door.

"Regrets?" Chasen said lazily, without moving.

"Nope. I just have a situation at work," he said.

"Okay. Talk later?"

"Oh, I'm sure we will," Delaney said, with a hint of sarcasm in his voice.

"Wait. What do you mean by that?" Chasen asked, sitting up quickly. "Let me see your phone."

Delaney shook his head, then slowly walked over to the bed and showed her the text from Marsh.

"Another dead body in the Charles. Meet at Community Rowing Boathouse in Watertown ASAP."

"Jesus. Another one? Let me get my stuff and I'll follow you over there."

"I'm not sure that's a great idea," Delaney said.

"Why? You don't think I can get ready that fast?"

She jumped out of bed and ran off toward the bathroom.

Delaney laughed. Most women he knew would have at least wrapped a sheet around themselves. Not Chasen. He noticed a butterfly tattoo between her shoulder blades before she ducked out of sight.

"Actually, I was thinking that it might look a little suspicious if you arrived so quickly on the scene, right after me."

He heard water running, and then the sound of someone working a toothbrush over their teeth with great ferocity.

Chasen said something garbled and mostly unintelligible, then poked her head out the bathroom door. She gave him a puzzled look, with toothpaste frothing around the corners of her open mouth.

"Why? I mean, it's not like we're dating or anything."

"Okay, fine. I'll see you over there," Delaney said, laughing again at her blunt appraisal of their relationship.

Excellent, he thought to himself, closing the door behind him. *So now I'm dating the chief coroner.*

He found his car where he'd left it on Charles Street, then grabbed a coffee at the 24-hour convenience store across from the Red Line T station and Mass General Hospital. The brown sludge was barely potable.

"Hey, Pop, this coffee tastes like it was made yesterday," he quipped to the elderly clerk behind the counter.

"It probably was," the man said, unapologetically, not bothering to look up. He was studying the obituaries in the *Boston Herald* with great interest.

"Anyone we know win the Irish Sweepstakes?" Delaney joked.

The old man shook his head slowly, still looking at the paper. "Someday it will be you, smart ass."

"Now that's a cheery thought," Delaney shot back.

"Have you found someone who'll marry you yet?" the guy said, turning the page to the wedding announcements.

"No," Delaney said, taken aback.

"How about that case on the Charles River; have you solved that one yet?"

"I'm working on it," Delaney said.

"Well, when you figure it out, I'll make you a fresh pot of coffee. Until then, give me two bucks and get back to work."

Delaney laughed and dug two dollars out of his pocket. He tossed the bills down on the counter, grinning all the way out the door. The affection between his father and himself had always been expressed in sarcastic volleys like this, and it seldom got any better. Even after his mother had died and his dad had gotten embroiled in an overtime scandal, Clancy Delaney was undaunted and as hardboiled as any ex-cop could be. Delaney felt badly that his father was now working at a convenience store, selling lottery tickets and crappy coffee right across from Mass General Hospital, but the old man seemed to take it all in stride. ("It's a job. It gets me out of the house, and if I die, the ambulance won't have far to go.") He should have been enjoying his retirement in Florida like the rest of his golf buddies, but he'd refused to implicate any of his fellow officers and been discharged from the BPD without his pension.

Delaney jumped back in his car and did a quick U-turn. He took Charles to Beacon Street and took a sharp right onto Berkeley, finally merging onto Storrow Drive West. Suddenly, the owl dream popped back into his head. He knew enough about himself to realize that his subconscious was trying to direct him toward something he'd missed. But what? Cemeteries, cedar trees, and owls had nothing to do with anything obvious. He mulled it over for a minute, sipping on the rotgut coffee. Stymied, he started thinking about Sue Chasen again, and how much fun they'd had last night. Suddenly he found himself smiling.

That was probably a mistake, he said to himself. Then he laughed out loud, nearly spilling his coffee, when he realized where this internal voice was coming from—his mother. If Siobhan Delaney were still alive, she would have never approved of this sort of woman as a potential partner for her son. After all, Sue Chasen was headstrong, liberal, and unabashedly opinionated—just like his mother had been.

Soon all his attention was focused on the simple but demanding task of weaving his way around Boston drivers. Rush hour had already started at 7 a.m., and people were scrambling into the city from the suburbs like a swarm of invasive beetles. Most die-hard commuters treated the four-lane highway like a racetrack, where lane lines were merely a suggestion. Thankfully, Delaney was heading in the opposite direction. The Charles River Basin soon appeared on his right, and the backside of Boston University lay just opposite—a row of red brick buildings with metal fire escapes. The sky was slate gray, and the heavy cloud cover offered little promise of sunshine.

Suddenly, a red motorcycle blew past him, doing about 80 miles per hour. Normally, he would have given chase, but he couldn't be bothered right now. It was probably some Boston University student, or a local kid heading off to work on a construction site somewhere, perhaps to rehab a wealthy person's McMansion out in the suburbs—someone like Sheldon Sparks. Delaney still needed to pay the multimillionaire a visit in Sherborn, to search his son's room and locate his laptop.

To do that, however, he might have to go back to the DA's office to get permission. He thought about how that might work for a few seconds, then got lost in the flow of traffic again. Boston was becoming too big, he thought, with too much development happening all at once. The roads just couldn't handle the volume of new housing being created on the periphery, and everything downtown was becoming gentrified. It was a double squeeze play forcing out the working class.

He pulled into the Community Rowing parking lot, just below the public skating rink in Brighton. It was still only 8 a.m., but the place was already bustling with activity. Rowers of all ages were coming in and out of the modern-looking structure, unconcerned about the cold weather. Who were these crazy people, he wondered, still out rowing in November? To the left of the elegant boathouse, he spotted a Brighton police cruiser with its flashing lights on, blocking entry to the public boat ramp.

As he got closer, he could see the patrol officer talking with a familiar woman in a red jumpsuit. Another woman was idling in an aluminum launch, several feet offshore. She seemed to be assisting in some way, pushing at something with a long oar. Then he saw it, rolling over like a submerged log. With some difficulty, the Brighton cops pulled the body from the river and placed it on a gurney—a scruffy-looking man wrapped in a long, tattered overcoat.

Despite the cold water, the decomposing body smelled strongly, and everyone quickly took a few steps back.

"We've got to stop meeting like this," Sue Chasen said, covering the smug expression on her face with a white medical mask.

"Okay, so how did you get here before me?" Delaney said.

"Motorcycle," she said, pointing toward the parking lot. He looked over and saw the shiny red Ducati.

"So, you're the one who just blew by me doing 80," he said. "I should give you a speeding ticket."

"Don't you have to catch me first?" she teased.

"I believe I already did," Delaney shot back.

"Not even close. By the way, I just met your partner."

"Who?"

Suddenly, Delaney heard an all too familiar voice behind him.

"Hi, boss. Did you get my text?" Marsh said.

"Obviously," Delaney replied.

"Hey, Sean, is this your lady friend?"

"No, Marsh. This is Sue Chasen, the chief coroner. She's here to look at the body."

Delaney caught himself speaking slowly and clearly, as if he were talking to a 10-year-old.

"Oh, okay," Marsh said, looking down at the corpse. "Because I thought maybe she was your lady friend."

"Please remove that idea from your brain, Marsh. And by the way, no one says 'lady friend' anymore," Delaney said, getting a little annoyed. The last thing he needed was for his partner to start circulating a rumor around the barracks about his budding romance.

"Well, I suppose we *are* friends," Chasen teased. "And I am a lady."

Marsh grinned with approval.

"All right, can we get to work here?" Delaney said. "What's going on with the stiff?" he said, nodding toward the body.

"Well, he's clearly been in the soup for a while, based on how badly decomposed the body is," Chasen said, as she knelt to examine the corpse. "I see no obvious marks to indicate foul play, but I'll have to get a better look back at the lab."

"Looks like a homeless person," Delaney said. "Who found him?"

"The lady in the boat, over there," Marsh said, pointing. The young coach waved from the launch. She looked scared and shaken up. Her first dead body.

"Okay, Marsh, take her statement and let's wrap it up and get this body in the meat wagon before the news trucks arrive."

The media was going to have a field day with this second fatality, and Delaney was already calculating how he could spin it. He'd already decided in his mind that this death, which must have occurred weeks ago, probably didn't connect with the other one. He didn't know why, but his gut told him so. He started to walk back to his car, then spun back around.

"Let me know if you find any tattoos on the body," he barked.

"Aye, aye, Captain," Chasen said. Marsh smiled again. Then, suddenly, it started to rain.

"Have a nice ride back on your bike," Delaney added, holding out his hand to indicate the precipitation.

"Will do. I'll make sure I stay under the speed limit," Chasen said.

Delaney shook his head. Knowing Chasen, her jumpsuit was probably fully waterproof. He jumped into his car and dialed the main number of the barracks. Then he asked the dispatcher for IT.

"DeFavio here," the voice said.

"Hey, Anthony," he said. "Any luck with that cellphone data recovery?"

"Nothing yet. It's pretty badly damaged, I'm afraid."

"Okay, keep me posted. Meanwhile, dig up anything you can on owls."

"Owls?" DeFavio said. "Like what?"

"Not sure. Focus on the owl tattoo that Finley Sparks had on his arm. I want to know where it came from, or if there's anything particular about that design."

"Okay, but that's pretty random, Sean."

"Life is random, Anthony. Murder generally isn't."

"Are we feeling a little philosophical today or just in a bad mood?" DeFavio asked.

"Maybe just a little desperate for a lead," Delaney admitted, ending the call to take another.

"Hey, why did you run off so fast?" the woman's voice said. He spotted Sue Chasen, standing under a tree along the Charles, looking directly at him.

"Sorry. I'm working on a lead," he said. "And Marsh kind of drives me nuts."

"Something to do with tattoos?"

"Just a hunch. I had a dream about owls and cemeteries last night."

Chasen laughed. "It's good to know that I inspire such beatific visions."

"I think the owl tattoo might be significant," he said. "I just don't know why."

"Okay," Chasen said, waiting for more.

"Sorry. I don't want to talk about it too much right now while my brain is trying to process different bits of information."

"Okay," she repeated, with a less inviting tone.

"I have a small brain, you see, so it's easily overtaxed," he added.

"Thanks for sharing," Chasen laughed. "I guess that makes everything better."

"Which part? My small brain or my need for quiet?"

"Both. I mean, the last thing I need is some smart-ass guy hanging around me who talks too much."

Delaney laughed. "Okay. You have a nice day, Chief Coroner."

"You too, Inspector."

Delaney started his engine and drove off into the rain, flicking on his wipers as he exited from the public parking lot. The wipers badly needed replacing, and the rain streaked across his windshield in a sloppy mess, making visibility poor.

He carefully reentered the flow of morning traffic, and then thought about the second body, dragged out of the Charles like a dead fish. It might be a homeless guy who had nothing to do with the case. Then again, they couldn't just dismiss him. This was a man, after all, who'd had a life too, and somehow ended up in the same river as Finley Sparks.

One thing was certain. Water was everywhere, getting into everything and everyone.

Delaney found a spot on the windshield where he could see forward clearly, by leaning slightly over to his right. That bothered his back a little, though, from an old football injury. It was going to be that sort of a day.

· 10 ·

Infamy

"*Y*ou might be interested in this one," Linda Matthews said, stopping Delaney as he walked past her dispatch station. "A female Harvard student just called in, claiming some creep on the shore exposed himself to her while she was out rowing this morning."

"Ooh, a flasher!" said Anthony DeFavio. He was leaning up against the dispatch station, checking his cellphone. He didn't bother to look up, even as Marsh McDonald wandered through the front entryway and joined them, eager for the news.

"Did someone say *Flashdance*?" he asked. "That was one of my favorite movies!"

DeFavio laughed.

"Where was the perp located?" Delaney said, ignoring DeFavio and Marsh and their juvenile banter.

"Just above the Eliot Bridge, on the Cambridge side," said Matthews, reading from her note pad.

"It was probably in the gay forest," DeFavio offered.

"Come again?" Linda Matthews said.

"It's a little clump of woods where men hook up," Marsh explained.

"What did you call it?" Matthews persisted, with a reproachful tone in her voice.

"Sorry. That's what it was known as when we were kids. Don't get all PC on me, Linda!" DeFavio said.

Matthews was still frowning.

"Did you guys attend the gender discrimination workshop last week?" she asked. DeFavio looked over at Marsh, and they both shrugged.

"Yeah, I was there."

"Linda, can't the Harvard police field that call?" Delaney said, cutting short the office squabble.

"Or someone else on patrol?" He briefly looked at Marsh, then over at DeFavio, who were now working their phones like they were slot machines.

"Can't you see we're busy?" DeFavio responded. "Research."

Matthews and Delaney exchanged a look of disdain.

"Okay, fine. I have to head over to Cambridge anyway to track down a lead on those oars that were reported missing last weekend."

"Do you think they might have something to do with the case?" Matthews asked.

Delaney shrugged. "Who knows? A lot of weird things seem to be happening on the Charles River these days."

"Maybe it's just a coincidence," Matthews said.

"Or maybe not," Marsh added.

"Hey, Anthony, don't go blind looking at that thing, okay?" Delaney said, glancing back at the IT specialist, who was totally engrossed in his computer screen.

"What?" DeFavio asked.

"Never mind."

Delaney and Matthews exchanged a parting smile.

* * * * *

The Harvard graduate student was waiting for Delaney just outside the main entryway of the JFK School of Government. She looked to be in her mid-20s, smartly dressed, with a leather book bag slung over her shoulder. They exchanged pleasantries and he displayed his badge. Then they sat down at one of the outdoor tables in the front courtyard.

"So can you give me a description of the guy?" Delaney asked.

"Uh, I don't know," she said. "I didn't get a close look at his face."

"Okay, well, middle-aged? Young? Light-skinned? Dark?"

"White and middle-aged," she said, looking the policeman up and down as if using him as a template for comparison. "I think he was wearing gray sweatpants and a hoodie," she offered.

"Okay. Is that all you can remember?"

She nodded, smiling politely.

"Okay. If we happen to catch the guy, would you like to file a formal complaint?"

She shrugged. "I'm not sure about that. All I know is that it's happened twice now, so I figured I ought to report it."

"It happened twice?" Delaney asked.

"Yeah, the first time was probably a few weeks ago," she explained.

"In the same place?"

The young woman nodded.

"So just out of curiosity, how come you didn't call it in the first time?"

"Well, I did call the Harvard police," she said.

"You did? Oh, okay. That's good," Delaney said. "You did the right thing." He mulled this information over for a second. "By any chance, do you remember the campus officer you spoke with?"

The young woman frowned, then shook her head.

"He was big—bigger than you. And older, too. Gray hair. He was nice."

"Okay, great," Delaney said. "I think I know who you mean. Here's my card if you remember anything else about the incident. Otherwise, I hope the rest of your day goes better."

"Thanks," the graduate student said, as they both stood up. She gave him a guarded smile, and then paused, staring at him, as if she'd never seen a state trooper up close before.

Walking back toward his cruiser, Delaney spotted a group of Kennedy school students playing Frisbee on the grassy area which lay adjacent to the school. Ah, college students, he thought. Most of them had a casual way of going about their day that he almost envied. Strolling from one campus building to the next, they reminded him of tourists at Disneyland, insulated from real life. Yet outside that gated community was a scary world of shady people that hopefully most of them would only encounter on television or in bad dreams. And it was Delaney's job to keep it that way.

* * * * *

His Ford Explorer was parked in front of Charlie's Kitchen, one of the few original eateries still left in Harvard Square. The smell of grilled hamburgers and steak fries wafted out of the open doorway, suddenly reminding Delaney of his teenage days when he and his friends hung out near the Harvard Square newsstand during the day, and then ran around, seeing what buildings they could break into at night. Harvard University hadn't changed all that much, but everything else around it certainly had, himself included.

On a whim, he decided to walk over to the campus police department, even though it was several blocks away. With all the one-way streets and lack of parking in Harvard Square, Delaney knew that he'd make better time on foot. Besides, he had a sudden urge to see how many of his old haunts were still there, 20 years later. Strolling up Brattle Street, he immediately spotted Cardullo's Gourmet shop on his left, just before the 90-degree bend in the road formerly marked by Nini's corner newsstand. Delaney crossed the three-way intersection in front of the Harvard Coop, merging on to Mass Avenue. The original Tasty sandwich shop, where he'd enjoyed endless burgers and milkshakes, had been replaced by a CVS drugstore, flanked by a Starbucks. The Wursthaus, which had once served bratwurst and imported beer, had been replaced by a "contemporary" restaurant called the Russell Tavern.

Fortunately, not everything had changed. A few blocks further along Mass Avenue, Delaney spotted the old Leavitt & Peirce building, with its trademark Indian maiden figurehead projecting from billboards advertising "Gifts, tobacco, and games." Floor-to-ceiling windows beckoned to the curious passerbys, displaying everything from perfumed soaps to hookah pipes—exotic wares that were a pleasure to look at, if not to buy.

Normally, Delaney would steer clear of the place, having no reason to step inside, but something in the window case caught his eye. It was a simple 8" × 10" sheet of paper, tacked to the side wall of the display case. A handwritten list of names, labeled 1–8, as well as a ninth spot labeled "coxswain." Even though he was just learning about rowing, Delaney was able to decipher the hieroglyphics: It was an old Harvard crew lineup from 2010, left up on the wall for posterity. It helped, of course, that the coxswain's name was now quite familiar to him.

Stepping inside, Delaney was quickly assaulted by the smell of exotic tobacco. The thick, resinous odor permeated the entire room. Large glass canisters lay in front of the main counter, holding loose leaf brands of every possible ilk, as well as cigars and smoking paraphernalia. On the opposite side of the room there were glass cases displaying pipes of various shapes and sizes. But the store was not just about smoking; it was half museum, half curiosity shop. Squeezed together on a center island lay a mishmash of colorful knickknacks, from marbles to shaving cream, pocketknives to chess sets. Other forgotten board games, like Parcheesi, were there, that most young people had never heard of before. And running along the painted, beadboard walls hung historic photos, primarily of famous sporting teams and icons long gone by. He spotted the crossed hockey sticks of Billy and Bob Cleary with their black-and-white photos from their epic 1960 Squaw Valley Olympics defeat of the Russians; and on the opposite wall near an old Chesterfield placard were a set of old wooden oars and team photos of Harvard crews from the early 1900s. One of the photographs suddenly caught his eye. It was a more recent shot, taken in color.

"The Infamous Harvard Crew of 2010," a descriptive placard read. He took out his iPhone and took a shot of it.

The coxswain's name was Finley Sparks; the store was selling copies of the team photo for $20.

* * * * *

Bob Rousseau's office was on the top floor of a nondescript brick building on Mass Avenue, marked by a simple blue light on the outer wall near the entry door. Delaney hit the intercom button and, without ceremony, he was immediately buzzed into a tiny foyer with a single, three-story elevator. It was a no frills building inside and out, the sort of building where you might expect to find an insurance agency or a dentist's office.

College police departments provided the first line of defense for any unlawful activity taking place on campus, but they also dealt with a whole range of other issues that took place within the boundaries of the university, from drunken students to providing extra security for visiting dignitaries or their sons and daughters. By and large, the staff was composed of retired cops who wanted a less stressful life for themselves. A couple of older guys from the BPD had landed there, including Lieutenant Bob Rousseau.

Stepping off the elevator, he spotted a glass door, behind which lay a desk where the dispatch officer sat. Delaney flashed his badge, and politely asked if the police chief was in. Before they had time for small talk, the inner door opened.

"Sean Delaney," Rousseau said, "What a pleasant surprise." The two officers briefly shook hands. "To what do I owe the pleasure?"

"I just happened to be in the neighborhood," Delaney lied, smiling at Rousseau and then back at the dispatch officer.

"Come on inside," the lieutenant said, sensing the need for discretion.

The chief ushered Delaney down a short hallway and back to a tiny office. Despite lack of space, it had a terrific bird's-eye view of the Charles River and the main campus. The walls were adorned with various awards and old photos, including an old black-and-white of Rousseau's father, who ran the homicide division of the Boston police back in the 1950s. Delaney couldn't help but think of his own father, and how he'd been disgraced.

"So, what's on your mind?" Rousseau said, pointing to a chair.

"Well, I was just speaking with a co-ed over at the Kennedy School," Delaney began.

"Amazing place," Rousseau said. "Do you know that Barack Obama went to school there before he became president? Rumor has it that he ran up quite a collection of unpaid parking tickets." He paused to laugh, despite Delaney's flat reaction. "Who would've guessed that years later I'd be assigning a security detail for his daughter when she came here as an undergrad!"

Delaney smiled and nodded amiably.

"Bob, the student I interviewed told me that she'd reported an incident of indecent exposure to your office a few weeks ago," he said.

"Oh?" Rousseau said. "Why are you interested in that?"

"Because it happened again, and this time she called our dispatch number."

"Oh? Yes, I think I do remember something about that incident now. It happened off campus, I believe, while she was out rowing?"

"Up near the Eliot Bridge," Delaney said.

Rousseau folded his large hands together comfortably in his lap and smiled. "Yes, I seem to recall that we had a cruiser swing by the area but didn't find anything."

"And there was no follow-up?"

"Well, Sean, as you so kindly pointed out to me a week ago, the Charles River isn't really our domain beyond the campus boundaries," Rousseau said, referring to their previous interaction at the BU Bridge, where Finley's body had been recovered.

Delaney smiled back. "Okay I might have been a little out of line there, although to be fair you did make a crack about F Troop, and that was pretty close to the bone."

"Apology accepted," Rousseau said, smiling. "How's your father doing, anyway?"

"He's fine," Delaney lied.

The two men looked at each other for a moment in silence.

"Look, Bob, I'm not here to dig up ancient history," Delaney said. "I don't care why you were at the murder scene, or why you didn't follow up with the grad student. I'm just trying to rule out that this indecent exposure incident had any connection with the suspicious death of that ex-Harvard student."

"Finley Sparks? So now the drowning is being treated as a homicide?" Rousseau asked.

Delaney gave a noncommittal nod. Technically, he wasn't supposed to reveal anything about the case, but it couldn't hurt to throw the lieutenant a bone. After all, it was better to have Rousseau on his side than for the two of them to be working at cross purposes, particularly since the Harvard police chief and Sheldon Sparks were obviously friends.

"Honestly, Sean, I just showed up at the river that day as a favor for the old man. But I doubt this indecent exposure incident has anything to do with the homicide. If I were you, I'd focus on that crew coach."

"Yeah, that's what everyone keeps telling me," Delaney laughed. He stood up to leave, extending his hand to his colleague. Then he took one last look out of Rousseau's window, admiring the picturesque view of the Harvard campus and the river beyond.

"I'm totally jealous," he said, motioning at the window. "My office has a view of Storrow Drive."

Rousseau laughed. "I guess being a campus cop does have its privileges."

Indeed, it does, Delaney thought, walking toward the elevator. Like knowing who the victim is before he is pulled out of the water (*I just showed up at the river to do a favor for the old man*). And more importantly . . . how did Sheldon Sparks know that his son had drowned, prior to his body being identified?

· 11 ·

Town and Gown

$\mathcal{D}$elaney drove down Mount Auburn, then turned left onto Ash Street, heading back toward the river. At Memorial Drive he took a right, put on his flashers, and slowly cruised upstream, scanning the riverbanks for any pedestrians who fit the vague description of the man who had exposed himself to the Harvard student. When he got to Gerry's Landing Road, he passed by the Cambridge Boat Club and the Buckingham, Browne, and Nichols School, then did a quick U-turn and pulled into the parking lot of the American Legion Marsh Post.

The building was a simple red brick structure that looked like it had seen better days, but it sat on a piece of prime river real estate. Just above it was the Belmont Hill and Winsor School Boat House, nestled in the small, wooded area that DeFavio and Marsh had talked about this morning. The only car in the parking lot was a white step van that looked old and abandoned. Delaney gave it a quick look and then followed the bike path under the Eliot Bridge, where homeless people sometimes found shelter. The tunnel smelled of urine, but it was currently unoccupied.

On the other side of the bridge, he walked up to the Cambridge Boat Club boathouse and rang the front bell. A man came out, holding a cellphone to his ear, and indicated that he was Mitch Jones, the director of the Head of the Charles Regatta. They'd already spoken about the missing oars. He let Delaney inside, where the smell of old varnished wood permeated the air. Still talking on his phone, Jones led him through the building and out onto an elegant wraparound porch that had a panoramic view of the river.

"That's where the oars were stolen," he said, pointing to a small lawn on the side of the boathouse. "Sorry, I've got to take this call," he apologized.

Delaney nodded and walked down the dock, making his way toward the water and then over to the grassy area. A lone sculler went by, making slow progress against the wind. Oars and boats lay around, neatly racked.

"Is this outdoor gate always kept locked?" he called back at Jones, who was still on the boathouse porch, talking on his phone.

The man gave him a thumbs up but didn't interrupt his call. After a few minutes looking around, Delaney had seen enough.

"Thanks for your help," he shouted to Jones. "I'll let myself out."

The man gave a brief wave and kept on talking.

Delaney exited the building and slowly made his way back to his cruiser. Someone who didn't have time for him wasn't going to get his full attention either.

Back on the other side of the bridge, he took a short walk through the little forest, noting a few homeless encampments that were currently unoccupied. Otherwise, the woods seemed utterly devoid of life. Delaney stood for a second and then looked out at the river, which was not yet cold enough to freeze. Still, the water had a feeling of heaviness to it, and he picked up a stick and threw it out into the middle of the Charles.

Oars, bodies, and indecent exposure, he thought. *What was the connection?* He briefly wondered how long it would take a floating body to travel downstream, but the stick went nowhere, held by the equal and opposing forces of the current and the wind.

"Nothing," he said to himself, and walked on.

The whole morning was beginning to seem like a total waste of time. But as he emerged from the woods, he suddenly spotted a man sitting on a picnic bench in front of the American Legion post. He had a hang-dog, unkempt look. An unlit cigarette dangled from his lips.

"Well, well," Delaney said. "If it isn't Ricky Miller."

"Been awhile," Ricky said, extending his knuckles toward Delaney.

"Fancy meeting you here," Delaney laughed. "Down by the banks of the River Charles."

"Love that dirty water," Ricky said. "What are you now, a big shot detective or what?" he added.

"That's right. Show respect."

Ricky Miller guffawed and looked Delaney up and down with a mocking leer. Delaney had known him back at Matignon High, when they were both frequently getting called to the principal's office. Ricky was just getting started as a petty thief, and Delaney was just figuring out how to stay out of trouble by taking out his aggressions on the football field. Miller clearly hadn't changed much over the years. He still looked as skeezy as ever, with a disorderly shock of black hair and crazy, silver-blue eyes. His entire body emanated cigarette and pot smoke.

"Jesus, Ricky, I think I'm getting a contact high just standing here next to you. Ever think of switching over to edibles?"

"What's that?"

Delaney laughed, and then the two sat in silence for a while as Miller casually lit up his cigarette.

"So, my friend, are you staying out of trouble, or still lifting bikes?" Delaney said.

Miller looked at him and tilted his head, like a horse that had just been shown the bit.

"What the hell?" he asked, laughing. "I thought we were having a friendly reunion here."

"Just relax. I don't care if you are or you aren't, I'm just asking the question."

"Yeah. And who wants to know?"

"So, I guess the answer to that is 'yes.'"

Ricky shrugged. "Whatever you say, Private Dick."

"Last weekend, the Head of the Charles," Delaney said, trying to get Ricky to focus. "You know, that rowing race with all the boats on the river?"

"You mean the one with all those little pukes pulling on oars?"

"Yeah. That's the one."

"Never heard of it," Ricky said, exhaling a blue plume of smoke.

"Very funny. So, you didn't happen to be hanging around here, scoping out some bikes. Or oars?"

"What? Me? Listen, I don't do that shit any more. No way. I mean look at me, boss. Do I look like that?"

Delaney just lifted his eyebrows. Ricky's clothes looked like they'd come from the Salvation Army. Instead of a proper winter coat, he had a ratty old windbreaker with a cotton hoodie underneath. He wore a pair of baggy jeans with black steel-toed boots.

"Seriously, check out my van over there," Ricky said. "I sell tools now. I'm totally legit."

He pointed toward the white step van, which had a Snap-On Tools' logo on the side. It looked like it had been built in the 1980s.

"Wow, that van looks vintage, Ricky. I didn't even know that company still existed," Delaney goaded him.

"Oh yeah, it's still around."

"So, if I was to look in the back door, I'd find tools, not bikes or drugs?"

Ricky threw the cigarette down on the ground, then stomped it out with the heel of his boot.

"Hell, yeah!"

Delaney laughed. They both knew that he used the van to transport stolen bikes and sell pot to high school kids. He also had a gift for talking his way into and out of anything. This skill came in particularly handy if you found yourself in prison, although Ricky Miller hadn't come out of his two stints in the Charles Street jail completely unscathed—he still had a dark scar under his left eye from the time another inmate tried to gouge it with a sharpened spoon.

"So?" Delaney said, staring at the scar.

"So what?" Ricky laughed.

"So, were you around here last weekend, during the Head of the Charles?"

"Yeah, like, I might have been there, checking out the rowing shit and the college girls," Ricky said, blowing out another billow of smoke. "Sometimes it's hard to remember one day from the next."

"I bet it is," Delaney said, handing him a $20 bill.

"Okay. Did you see anything weird?"

Ricky looked at him and laughed hysterically.

"Like what? I mean, you look weird; I look weird. The whole fucking world looks weird."

Delaney nodded. He had a valid point. After a while, nothing surprised you, no matter which side of the law you were on.

"Okay, relax, Mr. Policeman. I may have seen some fucking kids, horsing around under the bridge at night."

"That bridge?" Delaney pointed at Eliot.

Ricky looked at him, annoyed, and nodded.

"Okay. What were they doing?"

Miller shrugged. "Just messing around. Two of them were in an outboard, trying to paint graffiti under the arch."

"And were there oars in the boat?"

Ricky shrugged. "I don't know. It was dark out."

"Okay, thanks." Delaney said.

"So, am I your confidential informer now, or what?" Ricky asked, as Delaney started to walk away. He jumped off his perch and followed him toward the parking lot.

"Definitely not," Delaney said.

Miller laughed.

"Hey, I bet those rich kids ain't missing those oars too much," he said. "I mean, not that I steal oars or anything. I'm just saying—"

"Yeah, sure," Delaney said. Now Miller was baiting him.

At the end of the day, however, he knew that Ricky was right. Mitch Jones over at the Cambridge Boat Club would simply file an insurance claim and get a brand-new set of oars in no time at all. The bigger question was, where was a thief going to fence them? Or were they just going to hang them up on their wall for fun, like the ones on display at the Harvard Coop?

"Hey, Ricky, one last thing. Any chance you know a local guy who likes to drop his pants in public, near the Charles River?"

Miller laughed, then nodded. "Raymond St. James. Remember him?"

"You mean that weird kid in our neighborhood who never made it past eighth grade?"

"That's the one."

Delaney shook his head. St. James was a sweet kid, but he had the IQ of an eggplant.

"Incredible," he said. At least he'd solved one mystery.

"Hey, Delaney. Shouldn't you be investigating bigger things, like those bodies in the river I read about?" Ricky Miller shouted, as they both stood next to their vehicles.

"Maybe I am," Delaney said.

Ricky nodded.

"Love that dirty water," he said, laughing. He climbed into his van and started the beat-up old engine after a few tries.

Delaney laughed to himself as he sat in his Ford Explorer for a few minutes and checked the computer console for emails. *Ricky Miller as a confidential informant?* It was a crazy idea, but not an entirely bad one. He briefly looked at his phone and found a text message from Sue Chasen that simply said, "Call me." He dialed her number immediately. After hanging out with Ricky Miller, he longed for the sound of a normal human voice, without guile.

But when Sue Chasen answered, she sounded worried.

"Okay, so don't get mad at me, but I have something to tell you," she began.

"What? Are we breaking up already?" Delaney joked.

"Hopefully not. Are you sitting down?"

"Why?" Delaney said. "Now I'm getting nervous. Are you pregnant or something?"

"Be serious for a second."

"Okay, shoot."

"All right, I'm totally embarrassed to admit it, but somehow, they got Finley's blood samples mixed up at the lab. Turns out he didn't have anything except alcohol in his system. That, and a little cocaine."

"Okay," Delaney said, taking it in as calmly as he could.

"Sorry," Sue said. "This sort of thing doesn't happen very often."

"Well, the chief isn't going to like it very much. But to be honest, the whole Fentanyl piece has been puzzling me from the start."

"How so?"

"I don't know," Delaney said. "I guess it didn't quite fit the college-boy profile."

"I agree," Sue offered. "I only hope this doesn't mess things up."

"It's okay," Delaney said, his voice drifting off. He'd already started to readjust his thinking on the crime scene. "Let me chew on this and see where it leaves us, but let's keep this to ourselves for the moment. I'll get back to you when I figure things out."

"Okay," Sue said. "Thanks. And sorry again."

"Okay, talk soon," Delaney said, hanging up. He wasn't really that upset by Sue's revelation, but now he had to reshuffle the deck of details he'd been keeping inside his head. He also couldn't help thinking about the workplace cliché of getting involved with a colleague, and all the potential difficulties that lie within that sort of relationship.

On a whim, he left his car again and walked over to Eliot Bridge. This time he climbed the grassy bank near the VFW post and crossed halfway over the bridge to study the view below. He couldn't see any graffiti, even leaning out over the low brick balustrade, but the higher vantage point gave him a great view of the Cambridge Boat Club. It certainly had a unique position on the Charles River, right in the middle of the sharp elbow turn. He pulled himself upright again and noticed some missing bricks in the low wall, and what looked like a few splotches of red paint. The old bridge was in bad shape and certainly not up to code.

He dialed the State Police marine division, but no one picked up, so he got Linda Matthews on the line.

"Do me a favor, Linda. Call the marine division guys down at the locks and tell them to get a boat up under the Eliot Bridge."

"Okay. What are they looking for?" Matthews asked.

"Anything strange. Have them take photos of any fresh graffiti they find. And have them cover the top of the bridge, too. I'll text you a photo of what looks like a few splotches of red paint."

"Will do. By the way, we just got the go-ahead from Sheldon Sparks to search his son's room."

"Text me the address," Delaney said, suddenly energized. "I'm on my way."

· 12 ·

Lost in the Woods

"*I'll* do the talking," Sean Delaney said to Marsh as they walked up the long, winding staircase that led to the front door of the Sparks residence. The house was a simple but elegant Frank Lloyd Wright design, set back from the road and surrounded by a cluster of evergreens.

Delaney still couldn't believe that he'd been asked to swing back to the station and pick up Marsh McDonald, the cellphone-obsessed, millennial know-it-all. Marsh barely ever made it out into the field, and he was clearly better suited for research and office work. This was either the chief's idea of a bad joke, or Martinoli was sick of the young detective himself. Either way, Delaney didn't like having to babysit for the rookie. Driving out to Sherborn, they had already run into difficulty just trying to find the location of the victim's home.

"It wasn't really my fault we got lost," Marsh pointed out.

"It definitely was," Delaney shot back. "You were in charge of the GPS."

"Actually, you can't control a GPS. It works by a process known as triangulation, which means it needs to receive signals from at least three different satellites or cellphone towers to work correctly. Out here in the woods the signal is weak, so it's obviously prone to failure."

"Okay, Marsh, let's put it to rest. Like I said, I'll do the talking here."

The entryway path was lined with ferns, rhododendrons, and other bits of shade greenery, which seemed to complement one another perfectly. Beyond this, strewn about the expansive lawn, were some less successful attempts at landscaping. Stone sculptures stood among stands of white birch, looking like giant, naked bodies.

"This place reminds me of *Troll Master*," Marsh said.

"What the hell is that? One of those video games you play?"

"It's a movie, actually."

"A real winner, I'm sure," Delaney scoffed.

"Ouch!" Marsh cried out, suddenly pricking his finger on a climbing rose as he tried to ring the front doorbell.

"Careful, buddy," Delaney laughed. "We're not in the city anymore."

Delaney had never been to Sherborn or nearby Dover before, despite having lived in Boston his entire life. These were suburban enclaves where the superrich raised their young, drawn by the allure of country living, coupled with some of the top-ranked high schools in the state. Many of the more expensive houses, like the Sparkses' residence, were perched on several acres of land, equipped with swimming pools, horse stables, and tennis courts. Some of them looked more like summer camps to Delaney.

Back at the front gate of the residential compound, he and Marsh had been stopped by a security guard named Al, who gave them a sympathetic grimace when they held out their badges and mentioned whom they'd come to see.

"Christ, what's he done now?" the guy joked, pressing the button to release the electronic gate.

"I really couldn't say," Delaney told him.

"That's okay. Sometimes it's better not to know."

"Amen to that," Delaney said.

* * * * *

Sheldon Sparks answered the front door of his house, looking even more immense than Delaney remembered him from their first encounter in the assistant DA's office.

"Welcome to Sherwood Acres," he boomed.

"Thank you for letting us come over," Delaney said. "I know this must be a difficult time for you."

Sparks held up his hands and shook his head.

"I'll do anything I can to help," he said. "Come on in. Meet Athena, my better half. She does all the heavy lifting around here."

A young woman dressed in yoga tights and a striped T-shirt pranced down the staircase, barefoot and blonde. Based on the bounce in her step and her neon-colored toenails, Delaney pegged her as a second or even third wife.

"Sorry, I need to stir the bouillabaisse," Athena said, as if Delaney and Marsh had just arrived for dinner. She gave them a coquettish smile, then slowly padded her way across the bare wooden floor.

All the men were silent for a moment, as they watched her leave the room.

"She's an excellent cook and landscaper," Sparks said.

"It sounds like you're describing the help, dear!" Athena called out from the kitchen.

"Sorry," he shouted back. "She's got other skills, too," he said, lowering his voice and winking at the detectives.

"I heard that one, too!" Athena sang out. The tone of her voice was falsely sweet, bordering on a snarl.

"I was referring to your artwork, honey," Sparks protested. He rolled his eyes at Delaney and Marsh, then gestured toward some large canvasses which were splashed with bold colors. One of them faintly resembled an orchid, rendered in the style of Georgia O'Keeffe.

Marsh was still fussing with his injured finger.

"I'm afraid my colleague here just got bitten by one of your roses," Delaney said.

"Honey, you really should trim back those damn things," Sparks boomed. "I've told you many, many times."

"Relax, babe. I'll just get a Band-Aid for the poor man."

"Come in. Sit down," Sparks commanded. "Drinks?"

"No thanks," Delaney said.

"Of course. Straight to business. How can I help you?"

"Well, it would be useful to have a look at your son's room if that's okay, and any of his significant belongings, like a laptop."

"Of course, I'll take you right out to Finley's place."

"Out?" Delaney asked.

"Yes. He lived in the stables," Sheldon said. "He liked it that way—more privacy."

The three men exited the back door and walked across an expansive lawn filled with topiary and garden sculptures. A stone mermaid sat pining on a rock in the middle of an empty fountain which had been drained for the winter. Beyond that was a long outbuilding with vertical clapboards and a green tin roof.

"Mostly this is where I keep my vintage bike collection," Sparks explained, unlocking a reinforced metal door by punching in a code on a keypad. The he ushered the detectives into a long, narrow corridor of stalls, each of which held a beautiful motorcycle.

Marsh looked around excitedly, forgetting about his injured finger for the moment.

"Wow. Is that a Vincent Black Lightning?" he asked.

"Sure is," Sparks responded. "Want to buy it? I've got it up on eBay, and the last bid was only half a million."

He gave a throaty chuckle, looking to see if either man would respond.

"Where is Finley's room?" Delaney asked, unimpressed. He'd owned an old Triumph as a teenager and nearly killed himself several times.

"Right this way," Sheldon directed.

They passed through another door and into a small but elegant studio apartment. Afternoon sunlight poured in through a bank of high windows, illuminating a king-sized bed. A Hudson Bay blanket lay on top of it, drawn tight and smoothed to perfection. Nearby stood an antique desk and a small bookshelf. Overall, the place looked remarkably sparse and nondescript, except for a large exercise machine that sat right in the middle of the room, occupying much of the limited floor space.

Marsh bent down to examine the device, carefully moving the sliding seat back and forth.

"That's an ergometer," Sparks explained. "Here, let me show you how it works."

Before Marsh or Delaney could raise an objection, their host plopped himself down on the rowing machine, grabbed the handle, and started pulling furiously. Both detectives exchanged a glance of surprise as Sparks pounded away, making the flywheel spin wildly. But after only 20 strokes, he stopped, with his face as red as a boiled lobster.

"Christ, I used to be able to hit 1:30 splits," Sparks lamented, huffing and puffing as he tried to catch his breath.

"I thought your son was a coxswain," Delaney mused. "Isn't that supposed to be the guy who just steers the boat?"

"Yes. He was, but he also knew how to row. Everyone in a crew needs to know how hard it is to pull on an oar to really understand the sport."

Delaney nodded. "And did he always keep his place so neat and tidy?"

"Well, Athena may have straightened things up a bit."

"That's unfortunate," Delaney said. "Do you think your wife might remember what things she shifted around or removed?"

"I'll go ask her," Sparks replied, hoisting himself off the rowing machine. For an overweight ex-athlete, he still moved pretty well.

"Thank you. We'll just stay here and look around a bit if you don't mind."

"Sure, knock yourself out. Just don't steal any of my bikes," he laughed. "I've turned off the alarm system. Then again, they have no gas in the tanks, so you wouldn't get very far!"

Sparks trotted across the stables in his oversized khakis, kicking aside a tennis ball that lay in his path. It was often tell-tale, Delaney thought, to watch how someone moved about in their own house. So far, at least, Sheldon Sparks presented himself as a bit of mystery. On first inspection, he came off as an uber-successful, albeit boorish, businessman. He had a good-looking young wife and a beautiful house in the suburbs, filled with many expensive things. Yet despite all his bravado and wealth, his jerky movements and rapid-fire speech seemed to indicate someone who was ill at ease, or even unhappy. The dark circles under his eyes may have confirmed this hypothesis, along with the fact that Sheldon didn't seem as pushy with Delaney as he had been during their first encounter.

Then again, Delaney thought, *the guy had just lost his only son*. That would certainly unsettle anyone.

"See if you can find the laptop," he told Marsh. Then he circled the room, searching for other clues.

The walls of the apartment were mostly empty, aside from a few rowing photos, including a duplicate of the one Delaney had seen in the tobacco shop. In another, Finley and some of his Harvard teammates stood together, arms wrapped around each other's shoulders, posing in all their post-race glory. Most of them looked exuberant, but not Finley. His smile looked forced, like a little kid who'd been told to look pleasant. And despite his diminutive size, his curly brown hair and facial features largely resembled his father's—especially the look of hunger around the eyes.

Inside a small closet, Delaney found a random array of clothes and shoes. Ditto for the refrigerator. Everything was in order. Too much so.

"No laptop," Marsh said.

"Look under the mattress, just for kicks."

Marsh slid his hand under the bed.

"Bingo!" he said.

"Laptop?"

"Not exactly," Marsh replied, holding up a stack of old magazines. He set them on the floor and spread them out like a deck of cards. Each had a half-naked woman on the cover.

"*Playboys?*" Delaney said. "I thought that magazine had gone out of circulation."

"It did," Marsh said. "But these are really old. They're probably worth at least a hundred dollars each to the right person."

Delaney shook his head. "I don't even want to know how or why you know that," he said.

"It's common knowledge on the internet," Marsh replied.

Delaney held up a hand, silencing his partner.

"Well then, let me ask you this, Einstein. Why would a college kid bother with some old *Playboy* magazines when he could have access to online pornography?"

"That's a fair point. Unless there's no internet connection out here."

"I doubt it. Every inch of this place is wired. Think of those motorcycles and the security system in place."

"I have been," Marsh admitted, yielding the argument.

"Old motorcycles and *Playboy* magazines," Delaney mused.

"Seems pretty normal to me," Marsh said.

"Sure. Maybe if you're a 60-year-old, but not a 20-something."

Marsh shrugged. "What does that have to do with anything?"

"Everything is something," Delaney said.

He paced up and down the stables again, looking at the stalls and the bikes inside them. The converted stables reminded him of something, but he couldn't quite think of what it was. Suddenly, he heard the whirring of the ergometer start up again. He walked back to Finley's room to investigate and found his partner awkwardly trying to row.

"Marsh, what the hell are you doing?" he yelled.

"Sorry, I just wanted to try it out, boss."

"This is a murder investigation, not a joyride! Now get off that thing and help me search the rest of the room before Sheldon Sparks comes back."

Delaney shook his head and looked away in disgust, glancing up at a Harvard oar that hung on the wall over Finley's bed.

He stepped toward the bed, slid it away from the wall, and kneeled to examine the floor. Two fresh piles of plaster dust lay directly below the screw holes above it.

While he was there, something else caught his eye. The Hudson Bay blanket was a perfect petri dish, with its coarse woolen fibers that held onto everything. Laying upon it was a long blonde hair, shimmering like gold in the afternoon sunlight.

He picked it up, dropped it into a plastic evidence bag, and handed it to Marsh.

"See this? *This* is what we are supposed to be doing here—gathering clues."

"What did you find?" Marsh asked, mystified.

"Well, it looks like this oar has been hung up very recently, and someone with blonde hair has been sleeping in this bed."

"You mean Athena Sparks?"

"Either that, or it was Goldilocks," Delaney said. "But let's not jump to any conclusions."

As if on cue, the outer security door suddenly clicked open, and Sheldon Sparks entered with his wife. A blast of cold air flowed into the room. They were both dressed in shearling coats, and Athena had on a pair of Uggs.

"Well? Did you find anything?" Sparks asked, smiling. "Athena claims she hasn't been out here in weeks."

"Only these," Delaney said, holding out the stack of *Playboys*, as Marsh quietly slid the evidence bag into his pocket.

"Huh," Sparks said, with a mildly puzzled look. "I'm not sure what those were doing there."

"Relax, babe," Athena said. "Having a bunch of old girly magazines isn't a crime. Or is it, officer?"

She arched her perfectly plucked eyebrows at Marsh, then smiled coyly as she laid her head on her husband's shoulder.

"No, I suppose not," Marsh blushed. He grew silent and glanced down at his shoes.

Sparks snorted, suppressing a laugh.

"Well, are we done here, officers?"

"That's it for now," Delaney replied. "Thank you again. We'll just walk around the outside of the house to get to our car."

"Suit yourself," Sparks said, wrapping his arm around his wife's waist.

Delaney led the way back outside, with Marsh trailing along, taking one last glance at the motorcycles. As the metal door slammed shut behind them, it suddenly occurred to Delaney what the place reminded him of—a detention center.

"Sorry about that," Marsh mumbled.

"Which part? Jumping on the rowing machine or choking up in front of Athena Sparks?" Delaney laughed. He was suddenly in a better mood, having found a few clues.

"Something about her made me uncomfortable," Marsh said.

"What's the matter, buddy? Not used to dealing with a real live woman?"

"Not one like that," Marsh admitted.

"Well, maybe you need to get off that cellphone of yours, and get out more often," Delaney teased. Still, Marsh was right. Something was a bit off with Athena Sparks. Her flirtatious behavior seemed too forced. It was clearly an act for someone's benefit.

"Neither one of them seemed too broken up about Finley's death," Delaney pointed out, as he and Marsh got back into the car. Briefly, they listened to the crackling voices coming from the police scanner, just to make sure nothing too important was going on.

"I noticed that, too," Marsh said, finally composing himself.

"What else did you notice?" Delaney said.

Marsh thought for a second. "Well, the apartment had obviously been cleaned, aside from that strand of blonde hair and the plaster dust you found."

"So, Goldilocks is probably lying to us, and she *has* been out to the stables recently. But why would she leave those *Playboy* magazines around?"

"Unless it's not Finley who's been sleeping out there," Marsh speculated.

"That's what I've been wondering, too" Delaney said. "I'd bet money that Sheldon Sparks spends a lot of time in the doghouse."

"Or in the stables," Marsh said. "Maybe it's his mancave?"

"I'm thinking those *Playboy* magazines belong to him," Delaney said. "Did you notice how he wasn't very surprised to see them? Besides, anybody Finley's age would go online if they wanted to ogle naked women."

Marsh nodded. "So, do you think it's possible that Finley wasn't living at home at all?"

"Well, that would certainly explain why we didn't find a laptop or many of his personal belongings."

"So where was he staying?"

"Excellent question," Delaney said, starting the engine.

"I think it's time we returned to the Charles River and talked to some of Finley's ex-teammates. I'd like to know what he's been up to after graduating from Harvard, other than rowing on an ergometer."

· 13 ·

Mind Games

"Finley was into a lot of things," Brant Stillman explained. "Apps, cryptocurrency, video games—you name it. If it involved high tech and big money, he had his fingers in it."

Kyle Higgins, standing next to him, nodded. "He basically wanted to be the next Mark Zuckerberg."

Delaney, who was 6' tall in his standard issue boots, still had to look up to meet the eyes of the two ex-Harvard oarsmen, who stood 6'8" and 6'6", respectively. Stillman and Higgins were former teammates of Finley Sparks, and they'd agreed to meet the two detectives in Kendall Square, at the nondescript warehouse where they ran their video game company called Odyssey Rowing.

"So, Finley was also one of your business partners?" Delaney asked.

"He *was*," Stillman said, glancing over at Higgins. "Until we bought him out."

"More like pushed him out," Higgins grumbled, shaking his head. Despite a stylish man bun and a closely cropped beard, he didn't seem like a mellow guy. Minutes earlier, when they'd shaken hands, Delaney couldn't help but notice the power of the younger man's grip and his sharp, judgmental gaze. Stillman was more congenial and clearly the salesman of the two.

"Why the buyout?" Delaney pressed.

"He wasn't pulling his weight," Higgins said. "I mean, he had great ideas, but he'd quickly get bored and pass off the grunt work to others."

"In other words, the two of you," Delaney clarified.

"Typical coxswain behavior," Higgins scoffed. "Totally annoying."

Delaney nodded, then took a quick glance around the inside of the warehouse. It didn't look like much, outside of a few desks and unpacked boxes. In the center of the room sat a high-tech rowing machine, much fancier than the one he'd seen at the Sparkses' residence.

Bored with the preliminaries, Marsh McDonald had already wandered over to the machine and begun to inspect the large video monitor attached to it. *Please, don't sit on that thing*, Delaney thought to himself.

"So do you know what Finley was interested in recently?" Delaney said, then coughed a bit in the direction of his partner.

Stillman and Higgins looked at each other for a second, as if deciding which one of them would answer the question first.

"Well, this may sound kind of paranoid," Stillman offered, "but we think he was trying to pirate our virtual rowing game."

"How so?" Marsh asked, having mistaken Delaney's cough as a sign for him to join the conversation.

"Our theory is that he was trying to imbed some spyware into our system and gain access to the built-in camera, as well as any user's personal information."

Delaney shrugged. "Sorry, but you'll have to break all of that down for me. Maybe you can start by telling me how your product works."

"It looks like a combination of a video game and a piece of exercise machinery," Marsh ventured.

"Correct," Higgins said. "Go ahead and sit down. I'll show you how it works."

Before Delaney could object, Marsh plopped himself down on the machine and slid his feet into the foot straps, acting as if he knew how to row. Higgins began to demonstrate the various elements of the game to him.

"Someone who uses our Odyssey Rowing console basically enters an alternate reality," Stillman explained. "Envision yourself rowing through ancient vistas, facing challenges and battles like the warriors of old."

"Cool," Marsh said.

"Sometimes you'll row; sometimes you'll fight," Higgins elaborated, showing Marsh the alternate use of his oar handle as a weapon.

"You mean like Odysseus after the Trojan War?" Delaney asked, trying not to smirk.

"We actually started with that narrative," Higgins replied, "but then we expanded our repertoire. Now we also offer a *Viking Pillage* program and a *New World Conquest* game."

"Kyle was a classics major at Harvard," Stillman explained. "That and computer science, of course."

"Of course," Delaney said. He wasn't taken in by the sales pitch or the Harvard degrees.

Marsh, on the other hand, was completely sold. As he launched into a few tentative strokes, the video screen lit up and displayed him rowing on a Greek trireme. He and his crew mates were trying to outrun a malicious whirlpool that lay just off the boat's stern.

"Amazing," he exclaimed. "It's like *Guitar Hero*, only with oars!"

"Sure. Close enough," Higgins said.

"We believe that Odyssey Rowing will revolutionize the sport and the fitness industry in general," Stillman boasted.

"But I still don't understand," Delaney said. "What exactly is there to steal here?"

"Well, first off, if someone like Finley could hack into our system, they would gain access to all of the personal information our subscribers need to input before they play the game."

"So, your machine gathers and holds information, like Facebook or a cellphone?"

Stillman nodded. "And if you can hack into someone's account, you can lure them into all sorts of scams."

"Or even worse," Higgins added. "If you can gain access to the built-in camera, you can literally spy on people."

"How so?" Delaney asked.

Marsh stopped rowing, short of breath. A sea monster with several snakelike heads appeared on the screen, and he started battling it, using the oar handle as a spear. Delaney glared at him, but it was of no use; his partner was completely engrossed in the fantasy world.

"Well, a user thinks that they are just watching themselves row," Higgins said, typing some commands into a keyboard he'd attached to the back of the video screen.

"But in reality, someone else can see them, too, and record them," Stillman concluded.

Higgins hit a button and suddenly they were all watching a playback of Marsh rowing, looking more idiotic than heroic.

"Very entertaining," Delaney said. "But what can you do with a video of someone?"

"Oh, all sorts of things," Higgins said. "You'd be surprised."

"With a press of a button, this video clip could be all over the internet in seconds," Stillman added.

Marsh quietly got off the machine and tried to regain a professional demeanor. *Too late*, Delaney thought, glaring at his partner.

"That seems a bit nefarious," Delaney said.

"Well, Finley *was* nefarious," Higgins said. "But you're right, he probably wouldn't do something like that unless it was going to make money somehow."

"More likely, any personal information would simply be sold to third parties interested in tracking what clothes people buy, what care products they use, and other consumer-based behavior," Stillman elaborated. "Then he could suggest his own products."

"Okay, I get it, but there are federal wire-tapping laws that specifically prohibit the recording of people without their consent."

Higgins shrugged. "Technically, I suppose. Then again, some scientists over at Northeastern just uncovered the fact that smartphones do exactly this sort of thing, whenever someone uses their own video camera."

"I read about that," Marsh said.

Delaney was silent for a moment, taking it all in.

"So, if Finley did manage to hack into your system, I guess you guys would have been pretty angry with him."

"Sure, but not enough to kill him, if that's what you are suggesting," Higgins said.

"I'm not suggesting anything," Delaney said. "In fact, I don't believe either one of us even mentioned that Finley had been murdered."

Delaney glanced over at Marsh, who nodded his head in agreement. Both oarsmen were silent for a moment, suddenly looking less comfortable.

"We must've heard it through the rowing grapevine," Stillman offered.

"Uh-huh," Delaney intoned, with a trace of skepticism. "So other than you two, would anyone else on the team hold a grudge, or have any reason to do him any serious harm?"

"Well, our old coach lost his job because of him," Brant Stillman said.

"Not to mention his fiancée," Higgins added.

"Ed Masterson?" Delaney asked. "I knew that he lost his job after a frostbite incident. How did he lose his fiancée?"

"Oh, didn't you know? Finley's father seduced her," Stillman said.

"And then married her," Higgins added.

"Sheldon Sparks?" Delaney asked. "Wait a minute, let me get this straight. Are you telling me that Athena Sparks was originally Ed Masterson's girlfriend?"

"Bingo," Stillman said.

"And now she's Sheldon's third wife," Higgins clarified.

"Wow," Delaney exclaimed. "That's quite a game of musical chairs."

Stillman and Higgins both nodded.

"Do you guys still have any contact with Coach Masterson?" Delaney asked.

The two oarsmen looked at each other, then shrugged and nodded.

"Sure, we keep in touch a little," Brant Stillman said.

"Didn't he find Finley's body in the Charles?" Higgins asked.

Delaney nodded, noting that the tone of their responses had become more and more obliging since they'd discovered that foul play might be involved with Finley's drowning. His guess was that it was Masterson who had told them about the suspicious death line of inquiry.

"When I spoke to your ex-coach a few days ago, he seemed to imply that Finley was doing this sort of thing back in college—ferreting out other people's personal information as a way to manipulate them," Delaney said.

"Yeah, he definitely did," Brant Stillman admitted.

"It's called cyberbullying," Marsh offered.

"So, he was a chip off the old block," Delaney said, ignoring his partner.

"Probably, but he also learned some of that behavior from our rowing coaches," Higgins said.

"What do you mean?"

"Well, crew coaches know how to harass you in their own special way."

"How so?" Delaney asked.

Higgins shrugged. "There are various methods. They can tear apart your technique if they think you are being sloppy, or seat race you against another guy on your team."

"Seat race?"

"It's an inter-boat scrimmage," Higgins explained.

"Masterson loved to play mind games," Stillman said. "Of course, our head coach, Harry Parker, had perfected this behavior to an art form."

Higgins nodded in agreement, then smiled nostalgically.

"It almost sounds like you kind of miss it," Delaney said.

"Well, we definitely miss winning races," Stillman said.

"At Harvard, you learn how to win," Higgins emphasized. "It becomes addictive."

"Like video games?"

"Rowing is different. It's real," Stillman said, still basking in memories of his college rowing days.

"It's also totally nonviolent," Higgins pointed out, adjusting his manbun.

"Sounds idyllic," Delaney said, wondering how much time Higgins spent fixing his hair every morning. "So just out of curiosity, why did you guys come up with a game that seems to contradict the very essence of the sport you just described?"

Stillman answered. "*The Odyssey* is really designed for nonrowers; the game aspect is simply a way to get people who wouldn't normally row to give it a try."

"We also want to make money," Higgins said. "And regular oarsmen are notorious cheapskates."

"Let's get back to Finley," Delaney said. "What you are accusing him of is pretty malicious and done for his own personal gain. Do you have any proof that he was trying to hack into your system?"

"Not really," Stillman admitted. "But about a month ago, we started to lose a lot of subscribers, who told us they were no longer interested in the game."

"So, we did some digging and discovered a similar version of the software out there, offered on the dark web."

"That's an illicit part of the internet," Marsh explained.

Delaney scowled at his partner for assuming he didn't know about the dark web, which many criminals used as a kind of black market. All sorts of stolen goods and services could be found there, including credit card numbers, cryptocurrency, and even cheap Netflix subscriptions.

"So, you think Finley was having his cake and eating it, too?" Delaney asked. "Taking your buyout offer and then pirating your product afterward?"

"It fits his character, and this sort of thing would've been child's play for him," Higgins said.

"The gaming world is totally cutthroat," Stillman added.

"But not enough for someone to bump him off?"

Stillman shrugged. "Not us. We're oarsmen."

"Rowing is a gentleman's sport," Higgins explained.

Delaney smiled. It was good to see that the myth of social class and criminality was still alive and well.

"Well, whoever killed him obviously didn't play by those rules." Delaney nodded to Marsh and then toward the door. "We'll be in touch if we have any further questions, gentlemen."

He took one last look around the warehouse on his way out.

"By the way, do you have any security cameras in here?" he asked.

"No," Stillman said. "But Finley could have planted that software in our system before he left."

"Good point," Delaney said.

Outside, the winter air was dry and biting, and they could smell the faint but distinct peppermint odor of the NECCO candy factory over in Revere.

"Well, what do you think?" Marsh said.

"Those two don't seem like killers," he said. "They certainly have motive, and they're arrogant as hell, but I don't think they did it."

"Do you think they know who did?" Marsh asked.

"Maybe," Delaney said. "One thing is certain. This rowing fraternity is a tight-knit group, with some incestuous behavior going on."

"So, what's our next move?"

"I think I'll have another conversation with Coach Masterson and ask him why he didn't tell us everything about Athena Sparks."

"Shouldn't we talk to Athena Sparks as well?" Marsh said. "Maybe ask why her hair was on Finley's pillow?"

Delaney smiled. "I'll let you pursue that one, Marsh. I know you have a thing for her, but I'm not sure that's enough to treat her as a suspect."

"Well, she seems to be the only common thread in this case."

"And you figure if you pull on the thread, something might unravel?"

"Sure, boss. Something like that."

· 14 ·

The Catch

$\mathcal{I}$t felt good to be back out on the river again and back in his own boat. After only a week away from the Charles, Ed Masterson felt like his stroke had already gotten rusty, and it took him a full hour to get back into a groove. He watched the puddles of his oars fan out in pairs behind him, creating a pleasing circular pattern, which contrasted nicely with the straight unbroken line of his boat's wake.

Rowing on the Charles River on Thanksgiving Day was something of a tradition for Masterson, and he looked forward to it with the same enthusiasm that the L Street Brownies relished their New Year's dip in Dorchester Bay. The water had become denser in the cold, making the oars feel heavier as he rowed along. Soon ice would form, but usually not until January, and then he would switch over to his cross-country skis.

Despite appearances, sculling well was no small matter, and it required years of refinement to master. There were subtleties upon subtleties, most of which had to do with the successful marriage of fine-motor skills and raw muscle power. As he rowed along, approaching the Cambridge Boat Club, Masterson focused on the moment of connection between his blades and the moving water below them, commonly known as "the catch."

A perfect catch was always an elusive quest. You had to lift your hands quickly to set the blades, then wait for a split second until you felt the water grab them. Then you drove the oars smoothly and cleanly through each stroke, using your legs, back, and arms in perfect complement. He'd spent hours teaching this nuance to his Harvard oarsmen, because it was so critical to rowing well. But that was all in the past now, along with so many other things, trailing off behind him.

The surface of the river was littered with autumn leaves, and as he carved his way forward, some of the clusters got trapped underneath his hull, creating drag. Periodically, he needed to stop and take a few backstrokes to dislodge them, and he did so now, approaching the

117

boathouse. That's when he noticed the two detectives, standing on the dock with their arms folded, waiting for him to land. *Those jackass cops*, he thought, remembering the interview he'd been subjected to and the indignity of having his boat impounded. So, they wanted to talk to him again, did they? Well, they could wait a little longer, until he'd finished his workout. When they waved at him, he waved back. Then he held up two fingers and proceeded to row through the Eliot Bridge.

He already suspected what they were going to ask him about, because Brant Stillman had sent him a warning text that morning, adding the plea, *Don't tell them about the oars and the graffiti.* Why Stillman and Higgins had felt the need to sneak into the Newell boathouse during the Head of the Charles a month ago and borrow a Harvard launch was beyond him—all for the sake of putting their mark on the underside of Eliot. But people did odd things during reunion gatherings, often reverting to schoolboy behavior.

He glanced at the graffiti now as he rowed underneath it, the bold red letters said "H3V, National Champions." Why couldn't they have just bragged about themselves on Facebook, like everyone else, rather than defacing the historic landmark? On hot days in the middle of the summer, Masterson liked to stop and float under the stone arch to get a respite from the sun and to watch the light reflecting off the surface of water onto the dome of the arch. The underside of the bridge reminded him of a cathedral, cool and quiet and pleasantly dark.

Checking his oars in the water, he turned and crossed over to the other side, adjusting his point before sculling back through the Eliot Bridge. Bridges were like gateways to different sections of the river, and each one had its own unique character. Masterson knew all the sections of the Charles by heart, all the depths and shallows and currents and windbreaks. He didn't need to turn around very much or use a mirror to see where he was going. But now he had to deal with the detectives, and that required another kind of skill.

He made a perfect landing on the CBC dock, gliding in fast and then leaning away at the last moment so that his single scull pivoted into place. His dockside oar hit the legs of the younger detective, who was standing too close to the edge.

"Ow!" Marsh MacDonald said, hopping backward and nearly losing his balance.

"Oh. Sorry," Masterson half apologized. "I guess they don't call them hatchet blades for nothing."

"Those things really are dangerous," Marsh pointed out, rubbing his shins.

Masterson frowned. "What do you guys want? I hope you're not here to impound my boat again."

"Actually, we just wanted to talk to you about your ex," Delaney said.

"Athena? What about her?" Masterson asked, stepping out of his boat. Steam rose from his back as his sweat cooled.

"You never told us that she ran off with Sheldon Sparks."

Masterson unfastened his oars from the oarlocks, then set them down on the dock.

"Yeah. So what?"

He reached down and lifted his wooden single from the water, hoisting it over his head in one smooth motion. Both detectives stepped back to let him pass.

"So, that certainly gives you a motive to be angry with him."

"Sure. Maybe with the old man, but not with Finley."

Masterson started walking up the dock, carrying the long shell balanced on his head. Delaney and Marsh followed behind him, fascinated with how he managed the huge boat. Several steps later, he rolled his boat into slings, then found a rag and started wiping down the hull. The dark mahogany glistened in the sun.

"If you don't mind me asking, why did your fiancée leave you in the first place?" Delaney persisted.

Masterson chuckled. "Who said she left me?"

"So, it was the other way around?" Marsh asked.

Masterson puffed out his cheeks, then exhaled. "It was complicated."

"How so?"

"Well, let's just say that Athena wanted to spice things up a little, and I wasn't on board with all of her suggestions."

"Such as?"

"Have you heard of polyamory?"

"You mean multiple relationships at the same time?" Delaney asked.

"The more the merrier, as they say. She was a free spirit, which I only discovered after we were together for a while."

"So how did Sheldon Sparks fit into all of this?"

"Quite nicely, I imagine. He'd already been married twice, and after the party he invited us to, I made the mistake of telling Athena his inappropriate remark about her."

"And?"

"And I guess she found it, and him, intriguing. Or maybe it was just his money."

"What happened next?" Marsh said.

"Fill in the blanks, detective. She became the next Mrs. Sparks."

"But if she was such a free spirit, why bother getting married?" Delaney asked.

"I suppose she wanted to have her cake and eat it too," Masterson said. "Who knows? All I know is that I was out of the picture. Now I'm totally devoted to Alice."

"Is that your new girlfriend?" Marsh prodded.

"No, that's my boat," Masterson said, pointing at the bow where the boat's name was written.

After he finished wiping it down, he rolled the shell back over his head and walked into the boathouse, barely clearing the top of the low entryway. Delaney and Marsh followed him inside the boat bay, where it smelled of varnish, old wood, and paint.

"How did you and Athena first meet?" Delaney asked.

"At Harvard. She was a teaching assistant for a class in abnormal psychology."

"What were you doing in the class?" Marsh said.

Masterson smiled at the insinuation. "I was taking it for credit toward my master's degree in education."

"Oh," Marsh said, realizing his mistake. "Was it interesting?"

"It was, actually. I learned that we all fall on the spectrum between healthy and unhealthy behavior, depending on our circumstances in life."

"And where do you fall?" Delaney asked.

"Well, according to Athena, I'm obsessive-compulsive, but only toward rowing."

"Sounds like you didn't pay her enough attention," Marsh offered.

"That's probably true. Coaching demands a lot of your time, and if you're not involved with the sport, it doesn't make sense. Then again, when I started to hang out with Athena, I discovered that many of her colleagues engaged in some odd behaviors of their own. A few of them believed in UFOs, and others experimented with psychedelic drugs."

"Wow. I thought that sort of thing went out with Timothy Leary," Delaney said.

"What about Fentanyl?" Marsh asked, unaware of the false lab report.

"What's that?" Masterson asked.

"A high-powered opiate."

Masterson shook his head. "I get high on endorphins and Bud Light. Like I said, Athena was a little beyond me in certain areas. Maybe that's why we split up."

"Or maybe she just left you for greener pastures," Marsh opined.

Masterson glared at him with mild annoyance.

"Do you think Athena is still swapping beds?" Delaney continued, trying not to smile at his partner's impertinence. Still, Marsh was beginning to get the hang of good cop, bad cop.

"Not with me," Masterson laughed. "Like I told you, I'm not interested in that sort of thing."

"Well, would it surprise you to learn that we found what looked like a strand of her hair on Finley's pillow, over at the Sparkses' residence?"

"That could mean a lot of things," Masterson said, scratching his chin. "If you're asking me whether I think she was sleeping with Finley, I don't know. I guess it's possible, but that would've been pretty messed up—not to mention stupid."

"How so?"

"Well, if Sheldon ever found out she had eyes for his son, he'd go ballistic."

"Do you think he's capable of violence?" Delaney asked.

"I doubt it, but who knows?"

"And how do you think he would have dealt with Finley?"

"Not well. He's totally possessive. Like I said, he would have been quite angry."

"Enough to kill someone?" Marsh said.

"I doubt it, but how do I know? He'd probably blame the wife and shame the son. Or simply disinherit him."

As the trio stood talking on the CBC dock, the sun rose higher and began to warm up the cool November air. A few other scullers started to arrive, and Mitch Jones, the director of the Head of the Charles Regatta, came trotting down onto the dock, dressed in an oversized wool sweater, a pair of khakis, and penny loafers.

"Hello, detective," he said, smiling at Delaney as if they were old friends. "Are you here to apply for membership to our club, or just to bring me some good news about those missing oars?"

"Neither," Delaney said, returning a fake smile. The thought of him joining the private rowing club was almost amusing. He suddenly remembered the text he'd sent Linda Matthews earlier that day, inquiring about the Marine Division findings. A few days ago, he'd put in a request for them to take a launch and look under the Eliot Bridge for any recent graffiti and along the shore for any discarded oars. He took out his phone to see if she'd responded.

"Sorry, I hope I'm not interrupting anything," Jones apologized.

"It's okay, we're almost done here," Delaney said.

"What about Brant Stillman and Kyle Higgins, can you tell us anything about them?" Marsh said.

"Is that a trick question?" Ed Masterson said. "I mean, they were Finley's teammates and the stern pair of the boat he coxed."

"Excellent oarsmen," Jones chimed in. "They rowed a double scull in the Head of the Charles," he added. "If I'm not mistaken, they got second place."

"So, Stillman and Higgins currently row out of Cambridge Boat Club?" Delaney asked, growing more curious.

Mitch Jones nodded. "Members in good standing!"

"And do you think they could have been responsible for the oar heist?"

"Whatever for?" Jones laughed. "Those two have plenty of money to buy their own oars."

"Not even as a prank?" Delaney pressed.

"I seriously doubt it," Jones said, grimacing at the detective as if the suggestion was absurd.

As if on cue, Delaney's phone pinged. It was a response from Linda Matthews in the form of a photo she'd received from the Marine Division, detailing the underside of the Eliot Bridge.

"Can either of you tell me what 'H3V' means?" Delaney asked, holding up the photo on his phone.

Masterson and Jones glanced at it and then at each other.

"It's an abbreviation of the Harvard third varsity," Jones replied. Masterson nodded in agreement.

"And do either one of you know who might have painted it on the bridge?"

"Maybe, but I don't see how some old graffiti is relevant to your case," Masterson said.

"You can let us decide on that," Delaney replied. "And it's not old, it's freshly painted."

After a moment of uncomfortable silence, Masterson spoke.

"Okay, if you must know, I'm pretty sure Stillman and Higgins are responsible for it, but I still don't see how it's relevant."

"It's relevant because it places them right here, at the crime scene, on the night of Finley's murder," Marsh explained.

"We also have an eyewitness who saw a couple of guys in a launch right over there," Delaney said, pointing toward the Eliot Bridge.

Masterson shrugged. "I think it was probably just a dare that they did after their reunion row."

Delaney looked pointedly at Mitch Jones, then back at Masterson. "And was Finley with them?"

"How would I know? I wasn't there," Masterson said.

"Then how do you even know about it?" Marsh pointed out.

"Okay, they asked me how to access a Harvard coaching launch. Look, they're great guys. I'm sure they weren't involved in any serious wrongdoing."

"You mean, like defacing a bridge? Or murder?" Delaney said.

Masterson was silent as Delaney got on his phone and started calling the police dispatch.

"What are your plans for the rest of Thanksgiving weekend?" he asked the former coach, as the phone started ringing.

Masterson just glared at them.

"Well, don't leave town. We're going to bring in Brant Stillman and Kyle Higgins for more questioning, and if we find out they had a hand in Finley Sparks's death, you may be an accessory."

"Now that seems a bit heavy-handed," Mitch Jones objected.

Delaney gave Jones another pointed stare, then motioned to Marsh that it was time to leave. As the two detectives walked away, Masterson and Jones glanced at each other and then out at the river. They stared at the body of water for a while, as if they were just seeing it for the first time.

"What do you think, Marsh?" Delaney said, when the two of them were barely out of earshot. "Should I join the Cambridge Boat Club and take up rowing with all my leisure time?"

"Um, I don't think that guy was really serious when he invited you to join," Marsh said. He looked uncomfortable as he uttered the words. "I'm not sure he even likes you very much," he added.

Delaney laughed and slapped his partner on the back.

"No, he sure as hell doesn't. But I'm starting to like you, Marsh!"

· 15 ·

Entanglements

"Okay, tell me some good news," Chief Joe Martinoli said, sitting at his desk like a disgruntled Buddha. Detectives Delaney, McDonald, and DeFavio were all gathered in front of him, waiting to deliver their various updates.

"I think we're making progress," Delaney offered.

"Good, because I just got off the phone with the ADA, who is getting some more heat from Sheldon Sparks to hurry things up. Where do we stand?"

"Right now, we are looking at two ex-teammates of the victim who may have been with him on the night of the murder: Brant Stillman and Kyle Higgins. Honestly, though, I'm not entirely convinced they did it."

Martinoli lifted his eyebrows. "Really? That's all you've got?"

"There's also some funny business going on at the Sparkses' residence," Marsh McDonald added.

"Funny business? What are we, in second grade here?" the chief barked.

"Romantic entanglements," Delaney translated. "It might be nothing, but we're exploring the jealous husband angle as well. Sheldon's wife may have been playing around, quite possibly with Finley."

"Her own stepson? That sounds like a stretch," Martinoli scoffed. "Besides, if a guy like Sheldon Sparks got wind of something like that, he'd throw his wife in the river, not his son!"

"You haven't met Athena Sparks," Marsh said, smiling awkwardly.

Martinoli just stared at him and frowned. "What about the rowing coach, Ed Masterson?" he asked, shifting his gaze back to Delaney. "I thought he was our prime suspect?"

"He's clean so far," Delaney said. "We've grilled him twice, and he hasn't flinched."

Martinoli shook his head then turned toward DeFavio, who was sitting in his chair, entranced by his laptop.

"What have you got for me, Anthony?" Martinoli said. "Get anything off of that waterlogged cellphone?"

"Well, there was a lot of corrosion, but I did manage to pull a few texts and emails," DeFavio said. He glanced over at Delaney and Marsh and smiled, clearly pleased with himself.

"Okay, like what?" the chief said, impatiently.

"Well, there was a lot of texting back and forth between Finley and someone called Athena that caught my eye."

"Athena?" Martinoli asked.

"As in Athena Sparks?" Delaney added, with a hint of victory in his voice.

"Probably. I mean, how many women do you know with that name? Still, we should cross-check her cellphone number, just to be sure."

"I can do that," McDonald volunteered.

"What sort of texts?" Martinoli pressed.

"Corny stuff like 'the big, bad wolf is away, so come and play.' Could be some sort of code talk," DeFavio conjectured.

"Or maybe they were just playing Monopoly," Martinoli replied, still unimpressed.

"Any texts, calls, or emails with either Brant Stillman or Kyle Higgins?" Delaney interrupted, deflecting the attention away from his colleague.

"Only one," DeFavio said. "Looks like Stillman and Finley were supposed to meet on the night of the murder, but I can't quite make sense of the location. It just says Newell."

"What is that? A bar?" Martinoli asked.

"It's a boathouse," Delaney told the chief.

"The Harvard men's boathouse, to be precise," Marsh added.

"Well, shouldn't you be checking into that?" Martinoli asked.

"Marsh and I were just on our way over there to try and locate a launch that Stillman and Higgins may have used that night."

"Well, what are you waiting for?" Martinoli said, holding up his empty hands and waving them in dismissal.

Eagerly, the trio got up to leave, picking up their cheap plastic chairs.

"Stack them together neatly in the corner," Martinoli instructed. "And just so you know, I want this case wrapped up before Christmas, with a big, beautiful bow around the killer."

The chairs made a *thunk* as they stacked them together.

"Well, someone's in a great holiday mood," said DeFavio when they'd gotten out of earshot.

"Sure, a regular Father Christmas," Delaney replied, loudly enough for Linda Matthews to hear him. She was sitting over at dispatch, with her desk decorated in tinsel garland. A small artificial tree was perched on top of it, along with a stack of peppermint candy canes.

Marsh and DeFavio made a beeline for the candy.

"Hold on a sec," Matthews said to them. "Did either of you guys drop anything in the Toys for Tots donation box this year?" She pointed over at a cardboard bin, which sat near the exit.

DeFavio and Marsh both shook their heads.

"That's pathetic," Delaney said. "No treats for you guys."

On his way out, he grabbed a candy cane and started unwrapping the plastic.

"I saw that," Linda Matthews said.

Delaney just smiled as he popped the peppermint stick into his mouth.

· 16 ·

What the River Knows

"*I*sn't it funny how when you start thinking of Christmas, it suddenly appears everywhere?" Marsh McDonald said.

Delaney groaned. He was already feeling ambivalent about the season of giving this year, assaulting him with all its commercial and religious trappings; now he was saddled with a partner who was unequivocally obsessed with it. As they pulled off the Mass Pike and headed toward the Charles River, Marsh took it upon himself to point out every residence that was decked with seasonal decorations—from the most garish nativity scenes to brilliant displays of colored lights, elegantly strung in the limbs of barren trees.

"Look, there's Santa and his reindeer on top of someone's roof," he said. "You don't see that too often anymore."

"There's a reason for that," Delaney muttered. "It went out with Frank Sinatra."

"Frank who?" Marsh said. "Look, there's Rudolph the Red Nosed reindeer standing with all the other animals at the manger."

"That's nice, Marsh. Somehow, I don't think Rudolph witnessed the birth of Jesus."

"It's the spirit of the thing that counts," Marsh explained.

"Whatever you say," Delaney gave in. "Can we focus on the case now?"

As they merged into Nonantum Road near the Newton yacht club, they began to catch short glimpses of the Charles River. Patches of ice lined the shore there, turning silvery in color as the sun touched them. Driving by the public skating rink and Daly Field, Delaney thought about the second drowning victim, who'd been found nearby and finally identified as a local homeless man. He felt himself getting depressed. The chief was right; this case was getting cold. And now another New England winter was setting in, making it more difficult to locate clues.

"So do you think that Stillman and Higgins did it?" Marsh asked, snapping his partner back into reality.

"Not really, but there are definitely things they aren't telling us," Delaney mumbled, still immersed in his thoughts. "I also think we need to circle back and speak with Athena Sparks again," he added. "If Ed Masterson is telling the truth, she's not quite the dumb blonde she makes herself out to be."

"Look, there's a giant Frosty the Snowman!" Marsh interrupted, pointing toward a balloon figure advertising ice beer in front of Martignetti Liquors.

"I could sure use a frosty right about now," Delaney remarked.

* * * * *

The Harvard men's boathouse was considerably larger and more elegant than the cottagey looking Cambridge Boat Club they'd visited a week earlier. As Delaney and Marsh got out of their car, the two detectives took a moment to admire the stately, slate-shingled building. It was two stories tall, topped with an elegant gray-green roof that had multiple cupolas and ornate brass spires.

"Newell Boathouse," Marsh announced, reading from his phone. "Built over a century ago in honor of an ex-Harvard oarsman and football player named Marshall Newell."

"What was his claim to fame?" Delaney asked. "Other than being a two-sport athlete?"

"He was killed in a tragic accident a few years after he graduated."

"Christ, don't tell me he was found in the Charles River?"

"No. Run over by a train," Marsh said. "His college buddies raised the money to build this boathouse as a memorial."

"Well, that was awfully nice of them," Delaney said. "Do you think I'll ever get a building named after me?"

"I doubt it," his partner said, matter of fact.

"That was a joke, Marsh."

"Oh, I see."

The front door was open, so they entered the building and soon found themselves in a huge room filled with long rowing shells, laying horizontally on support racks. The interior space was dark and unheated, with only a bit of exterior light streaming in through windows at the front of the boat bays.

"Wow, these things are enormous," Delaney said, touching a tiny rudder on the stern of one boat that ran about 50 feet long.

"These must be the eight-oared shells,'" Marsh said. "I think they go for about 60 grand a piece."

"Almost as much as my annual salary," Delaney mumbled.

"Should we check out the second floor?" Marsh asked, bounding up the wide wooden staircase.

"I guess so," Delaney replied, following behind.

At the top of the stairs was an old black-and-white photo of Marshall Newell, the athlete for whom the historic building had been named.

"Looks like a nice enough guy," Marsh surmised.

Delaney shook his head and walked past his partner, entering an enormous, open training room filled with dozens of rowing machines. Massive post- and beam-support timbers underpinned the high roof line, boasting elaborate, old-school joinery. The sight was impressive, and as the two detectives walked around the perimeter of the room, they couldn't help but admire all the historic posters of Harvard crews and regattas gone by, dating all the way back to the mid-nineteenth century. Delaney had been in old boxing gyms before that had the same feeling as this, places filled with photos of former champions gone by, inspiring others to follow. One quote on the wall said it best: "Believe in yourself, and everything is possible."

Suddenly Delaney saw a photo of a coxswain on the wall, getting tossed in the water, and his reverie about the Harvard Crew glory days was broken.

"Okay, this is all very impressive, Marsh, but we're not going to find any launches up here," he said, coaxing his awestruck partner back downstairs.

They reentered the boat bays, where it was cold and damp. A small rat ran across the floor, seeking cover. On the periphery of the open room, multiple sets of 12-foot oars stood vertically up against the wall, their blade tips held in place by slotted racks. Everything seemed to be in its proper place, put away and stored for the winter. Something about the smell of the boathouse was familiar to Delaney. Partly, it reminded him of a summer camp he'd attended a long time ago on Squam Lake in New Hampshire. It too had a boathouse, but not as big as this.

Somewhere, off to their right, came another faint smell, more chemical and less appealing, along with the sound of a radio.

Delaney and Marsh moved in the direction of the music and found a sliding panel door that led into a workshop. An older man dressed in overalls and work boots stood inside, inspecting some Harvard oars he'd recently painted. The workshop was smaller and better heated than the boat bays. Cozy and cluttered, the room had two long workbenches, strewn with bits and pieces of broken rowing equipment and all the tools needed to fix it. In addition to a table saw, a bandsaw, and a drill press, there were various handsaws, clamps and smaller power tools, and jars of epoxy resin for gluing. Nearby, an outboard motor, half assembled, sat upright on a movable dolly.

Delaney displayed his badge for the boatman, who casually glanced up and nodded at the two detectives. The older man seemed unfazed by their appearance and finished the task he was working on. He removed a piece of masking tape from one of the finished oars, then reached over and turned down the volume of the radio. It looked like it was the same vintage as the oldies music coming out of it.

"You fellas following up on that break-in?" the boatman asked.

Marsh looked over at Delaney. "What break-in?"

"About a month ago," the man said. "The one I called the Harvard police about."

"Oh?" Delaney said. "And what did they find?"

"Not a whole heck of a lot, since nothing seemed to be missing," the man laughed.

Delaney returned an amiable nod. "We're actually here about Finley Sparks," he explained.

"Messy business," the boatman replied.

"How much do you know about it?" Delaney asked.

"Only bits and pieces. But enough to know that I don't want to know more."

"How well did you know the deceased?"

"Finley? Well, enough, I suppose."

"And what was your opinion of him when he was an undergraduate?" Delaney asked.

The boatman shrugged. "Typical coxswain—bossy."

"What about Brant Stillman and Kyle Higgins?"

"Typical stern pair," he laughed. "Even worse."

"I take it you don't like many people," Delaney said.

"I fix boats, not people," he quipped. "I leave that to the coaches."

"Okay. Tell me more about the break-in. How did you notice it?" Delaney said. He'd immediately taken a liking to the man.

"The back door was busted. Here, I'll show you."

The boatman, who finally introduced himself as Charlie Abbott, led them back through the boat bays and then into some indoor rowing tanks—an eight-seated simulation boat set into concrete, complete with oars resting in shallow pools of water. Long mirrors lined the two walls of the narrow room, angled down so that the seated oarsmen could examine their techniques as they rowed.

"Watch your step," Abbott barked at them, nimbly making his way along the narrow edge of the tanks to the back of the room, where an emergency exit door was located. Over his shoulder, he explained how this was where the teams practiced during the winter.

"Impressive," Delaney said, admiring the tanks. "You have to admit, Marsh. This is much better than any computer simulation device."

"I'll tell you in a second," Marsh replied.

Delaney looked back to see his partner sitting in one of the rowing seats, trying to figure out how to manipulate the oar.

"You've got your blade turned around ass-backward," the boatman said.

"Sorry," Delaney apologized. "He's a bit of a rookie."

"Clearly in more ways than one," Abbott chuckled.

They turned their attention to the emergency door, where Delaney found multiple scratches on the outer frame.

"Looks like they used a crossbar," he said. "Do you have a security system in this place?"

"Not really," the boatman shrugged. "There's not much to steal."

"What about all of those expensive boats?" Delaney asked.

"It would be pretty hard to move them without getting noticed," the boatman pointed out.

"So why would someone break in and then not steal anything?" Delaney said.

"Could've been a homeless person, looking for a place to spend the night," Marsh replied, rejoining them after his hapless attempt at rowing.

"Where does this door lead?" Delaney asked, ignoring his partner.

"Out to the dock where the launches are kept," Abbott replied. "I'm just getting ready to pull them out of the water for the winter."

The boatman led them outside, through a locked gate, and onto a massive wooden dock. The view was extraordinary, displaying a broad swath of the Charles River that upstaged everything else around it.

Giant sycamores lined the far bank, beyond which lay Harvard Square and the main campus of the university. Further off in the distance, Delaney could see a bit of the Boston city skyline. Somehow, this view of the river allowed him to survey everything around it from an altered perspective, where everything manmade was only a backdrop to the waterway. The Charles River was center stage. Smith led them down to the lower dock, where several powerboats were tied up.

"Anyone ever steal these launches?" Delaney asked.

"Sometimes. Mostly in the summer, to take a joyride."

"We have reason to believe that Stillman and Higgins may have borrowed one of them a few weeks ago."

"You mean the weekend Finley was found dead?"

Delaney nodded.

"Actually, this one in front of you hasn't worked since then, now that you mention it."

"What's wrong with it?" Marsh asked.

"Not sure," Abbott said. "I haven't had the time to look it over yet, but the coaches have all been complaining about it."

"Mind if I give it a try?" Marsh said.

The boatman shrugged. "Knock yourself out; the key is in it."

"Marsh—" Delaney began.

"Don't worry, boss. I might not be able to row, but I do know a little about engines."

Before Delaney could object further, Marsh hopped into the launch. He lifted the gas tank, noting that it was full. Then he checked the shift control, to make sure it was in neutral. Finally, he turned the key. The engine made a labored, whining sound.

"Plenty of juice in the battery," Marsh said. "Can we tilt the engine up?"

Abbott jumped on board, flipped a lever, and yanked the head of the engine forward.

"Well, I'll be damned," he said, looking down toward the prop, which was entangled with a piece of cloth, soaked with river water and dripping.

Delaney immediately recognized the crimson fabric. Putting on his latex gloves, he reached down and carefully unwound it from the prop. It was the same shade of red as the Harvard rowing jacket that Finley's body had been found in.

"Let's bag this," he said to Marsh. "And then call Linda and tell her to get a forensics team over here, right away."

· 17 ·

A Shot in the Dark

A lone figure stood on the parapet of the Eliot Bridge, gazing down at the river below. It was nighttime, and the video was grainy and blurred. A few streetlights barely helped the visibility, along with the headlights from a few passing cars.

Suddenly, the man turned, as if he heard something. It was difficult to see what happened next. He appeared to be talking to someone, gesturing at them with both hands. Then he lost his balance and fell backwards, dropping 20 feet into the water below.

There was a splash, followed by some bubbles, shimmering in the glare of a streetlight. The camera zoomed in, hovering. After several seconds, when the surface of the river was smooth again, it quickly panned left and right but found nothing.

After that, there was only darkness.

* * * * *

"*O*kay, do you mind telling me why we're in here?" asked Brant Stillman, glaring at Sean Delaney and Marsh McDonald. He and Kyle Higgins were sitting in the interview room of the state police barracks. All four men had hot coffee in front of them, steaming out of Styrofoam cups.

"Well, first off, we just found a piece of Finley's crew jacket and his DNA stuck in the prop of a Harvard launch," Delaney explained, watching closely to see how the ex-oarsmen would react.

"So?" Stillman said, glancing over at Kyle Higgins. His giant-sized business partner was studying the coffee in front of him with quiet disdain.

"*So*, according to your old coach, Ed Masterson, you guys 'borrowed' a Harvard launch to paint graffiti on the Eliot Bridge on the same night as Finley's death."

Stillman and Higgins were silent for a moment.

"And we're wondering if it's the same launch," Marsh added.

Stillman shrugged. Higgins opened his mouth as if he were about to speak, then adjusted his manbun instead.

"Look, if you guys know something, it's much better if you tell us now," Delaney said. "If we find out later, it won't go well for you with the district attorney."

"Okay," Stillman said. "We did see Finley that night, but we didn't kill him."

"Tell me exactly what happened," Delaney said. He tried to take a sip of his coffee and quickly put it down when it burned the roof of his mouth.

"Some of the guys from our Head of the Charles reunion crew were out drinking at the Owl Club that night, after the race. We'd put down a few beers and then Higgins and I got the brilliant idea to paint the bridge with a crimson H."

"You mean H3V?" Delaney clarified.

Stillman nodded.

"Was Finley with you?"

Higgins shook his head. "He's not a member of the Owl," he sniffed.

"Then why did he have an owl tattoo?" Marsh cut in.

"Beats me," Stillman said. "Maybe he was trying to impress his new girlfriend; he'd been bragging about her all weekend."

"Okay. What time did you leave the club?" Delaney resumed.

"About 9 p.m."

"Wait. Who was the girlfriend?" Marsh interrupted.

"He wouldn't give us any details," Higgins said.

"Okay, continue," Delaney prompted the two men.

"On the way over to the boathouse, Kyle and I started reminiscing about our graduation night, when we'd all jumped off the Weeks Footbridge."

"Really?" Marsh said, genuinely surprised.

"It's kind of a Harvard thing," Higgins explained.

Delaney just shook his head, unimpressed.

"Anyway, we suddenly realized that Finley had never jumped, so we called him up and started giving him a hard time about it."

"And?"

"And finally, we shamed him into it. He agreed to meet us at Newell and jump off the Eliot Bridge, instead of Weeks, since we were going up there to paint it anyway."

"But first you broke into the boathouse," Delaney said.

"We *snuck* in," Stillman corrected. "We used to row there, remember? It's like our second home."

"Except it's not," Marsh said.

"Anyway, Masterson had told us where to find the key to the launch in the workshop, and we grabbed a can of red spray paint while we were in there."

"Then what?" Delaney pressed.

"We motored up to Eliot to paint the arch. We dropped Finley off along the shore so he could take the plunge."

"Near the Cambridge Boat Club?"

Stillman nodded.

"Is that when you took the Harvard oars that were lying on the grass?" Delaney asked.

"How did you know about that?" Higgins cut in.

"Just a lucky guess," Delaney said. "Why did you steal them?"

Stillman shook his head, flustered, while Higgins's face had turned crimson.

"Look, we didn't steal anything," he said. "We were just returning the oars to Newell. They'd been loaned out for the regatta to a visiting crew that weekend."

"That's right," Stillman agreed. "We thought we'd be doing the regatta committee a favor, bringing the oars back to Harvard where they belonged."

"You guys aren't very good liars," Delaney said, smirking.

"What do you mean?" Stillman asked.

"Well, how come the oars never got returned?" the detective pointed out.

Stillman frowned. "Okay, there may have been some souvenir taking. Look, if you're going to treat us like criminals, maybe we need to call our lawyer."

"Relax," Delaney said. "Just tell me the rest of the story."

"Well, that's when things got crazy," Stillman said. "Finley was on the bridge, getting ready to jump. We were all set up to film it and everything."

"What do you mean, 'set up'?" Delaney asked.

"Finley wanted us to livestream the jump on YouTube so that everyone else on the team and his so-called girlfriend could see it."

"Naturally," Marsh said, looking at his cellphone.

"Please continue," Delaney said to Stillman.

"Well, Finley was standing there, on the edge of the bridge, but something wasn't quite right."

"How so?"

"Well, you're supposed to jump forward, feet first, to break the impact of the fall. Finley knew that, and we'd gone over the whole technique with him beforehand. But suddenly, for some reason, he turned around and hesitated."

"For a second he was hidden from view," Higgins added.

"That's right," Stillman said. "And then the next thing we knew, he came flying over the bridge, backward. When he hit the water, it didn't look good."

"We tried to rescue him with the launch," Higgins explained. "But the water near the bridge was dark, and we couldn't see anything. Then he was gone."

"What do you mean, 'gone'?" Delaney said.

"I mean, the body disappeared. It must have sunk."

"Or got caught under the boat," Marsh suggested.

"Okay. So why didn't you just call 911 right then and there?" Delaney asked.

"I don't know," Stillman said, shaking his head. "After a few minutes had passed and we couldn't find Finley, we thought we heard voices on the bridge and got worried that someone had seen us. We started thinking about how bad it might look, so we panicked and motored away!"

Higgins nodded in agreement.

Delaney looked quietly at the two Harvard oarsmen and slowly shook his head. Marsh was still scrolling around on his cellphone.

"I'm sorry, but what you've just described doesn't seem like the response of two innocent men."

"We were scared," Higgins admitted. "We couldn't find a body."

"I can understand how you would be," Delaney said. "But why didn't you tell me any of this before, when Detective McDonald and I came and questioned you the first time?"

Stillman shook his head. "I guess we were afraid of getting caught up in a big mess, and then falsely accused of something we didn't do."

Delaney unfolded his hands and stretched them forward. A wistful look came across his face, as if he were just noticing the wrinkles on them for the first time. Marsh was still glued to his cellphone.

"Okay, tell me why I should believe any part of this story." he said. "After all, you guys lied to me before and withheld evidence."

"Because it's *true*," Stillman said.

Delaney chuckled. "Okay, gentlemen. Here's what I think happened. One of you followed Finley up onto shore and then onto the bridge. Then you pushed him off when he chickened out and refused to jump. Or maybe you hit him over the head with an oar."

"No way," Stillman said.

"Maybe you didn't mean to kill him," Delaney continued. "Maybe you just wanted to scare him a little and get even for how he'd treated you over the years. After all, you guys are used to throwing coxswains into the river, right?"

"That's bullshit!" Higgins shouted. The giant oarsman's face suddenly reddened again. He looked like he might lunge forward at the detective, until Stillman put a steadying hand on his friend's shoulder.

"Look, it's true," Stillman said. "We didn't like Finley very much, but we had no intention of hurting him."

"You had means and motive," Delaney said. "That's how a jury will see it anyway, unless you can give me something else here."

"We've told you everything we know," Kyle Higgins pleaded.

"I'd like to believe you," Delaney said, softening his tone. "But, you see, one thing puzzles me about this whole thing. I'm not a waterman, so maybe you guys can help me out."

"What's that?" Brant Stillman said.

"You say that Finley fell off Eliot Bridge, and you couldn't find the body, so presumably he drowned."

"Correct," Higgins replied.

"And let me ask you this—is there much current in the Charles River?"

The two oarsmen looked at one another before silently shaking their heads.

"Not much," Stillman admitted.

"That's what I thought," Delaney said. "So, here's my question: How did Finley's body get all the way down to Magazine Beach, which is least a mile from the Eliot bridge. That's a long way to go if there isn't much current. Even if there was current, a floating body would probably get hung up on one of the bends before it made it all the way down to Boston University."

Brant Stillman gave a pensive nod. Higgins just stared down at his hands.

"Maybe the body got stuck under our launch," Brant Stillman speculated.

"Or maybe you ran over it on purpose, to finish the job."

"This is unbelievable," Higgins said. "What do you take us for, a couple of thugs?"

Delaney didn't respond.

"You said you took a video?" Marsh interrupted.

"We deleted it," Stillman said. "It's not exactly something we wanted to see again or have anyone else see."

"Really?" Marsh said. "Well, I just found it on Finley's Facebook page, and it looks like it just got put up recently."

"What?" Higgins said. "That's impossible!"

Marsh slid his phone across the table, and the two ex-oarsmen had a look at it.

"Well?" Delaney said.

"I don't know how it got there," Stillman replied. "We certainly didn't post it."

"Yeah. That would be totally sick," Higgins said.

"Who else could have done it?" Delaney said. "You two were the only ones who had the video, right?"

"Like I said, it was a YouTube livestream, so everyone on the team had access," Higgins explained. "We took it down as soon as we could." His voice suddenly sounded less certain, without all the arrogance behind it.

"Apparently not soon enough," Marsh pointed out.

Stillman bit one of his fingernails like a nervous chess player.

"Maybe that's not our film," he suggested. "Someone else could've been there that night, hidden from view."

Delaney shook his head. "Nice try, but now you're really grasping at straws. This video shows *exactly* what you described a moment ago, and it was taken from a position on the river just under the bridge."

"So what? That doesn't prove anything," Higgins said.

"I disagree," Delaney said. "I think at the very least you guys are looking at doing time for manslaughter."

Delaney nodded and motioned to Marsh, who stood up to escort Stillman and Higgins from the room.

"Wait! Are you arresting us?" Stillman asked.

"I think you'd better call that lawyer," Delaney said, as Marsh began to read them their *Miranda* rights.

After they'd left, he jotted down a few notes. Then he took a sip of his coffee, which had finally cooled off enough. Surprisingly, it tasted pretty good.

· 18 ·

Illusions

"*What* does a coxswain really do, anyway?" Delaney asked. It was almost Christmas Eve, and he was back at Sue Chasen's condo in Back Bay.

"You mean other than steer a huge boat with a tiny rudder?" she laughed, flicking on a blender filled with holiday eggnog. Delaney started rifling through her kitchen cabinets for mugs.

"Hey, do you mind?" she said. "We're not roommates yet."

"What's the big deal?" Delaney said. "I mean, am I going to find a dead body in here or something?"

"You never know," Sue joked. "Maybe one of my exes. Or maybe I don't want you to find out that I'm not very tidy."

She found two clean glasses and filled them up, sprinkling cinnamon on top. "Here, try this," she said. "And go sit down."

Delaney took a sip, then winced. "Wow, what did you put in here?" he asked.

"Just a bit of Captain Morgan's. Is that a problem, Sergeant?"

Delaney just smiled and shook his head, letting the sweet sensation of rum spread out into his cheeks and over his tongue. He'd been trying to reduce his alcohol consumption lately, but his timing was off with the holidays in full swing. It didn't help matters that he'd started hanging out with a woman who could drink him under the table.

As the inside of his mouth slowly grew numb, he wandered over to the living room and sat down on her sofa. Finally, it was time to relax. Back in the kitchen, Sue Chasen fiddled with her iPhone, trying to choose some jazz on Spotify. She finally selected *Kind of Blue*.

When the familiar bass and trumpet prelude began, Delaney felt himself relax. His mind began to wander freely, inspired by the modals of Miles Davis and alcohol.

"Okay," Sue said, plopping down on the sofa beside him. "I know you're thinking about the case, so just spill the beans. What's the latest?"

"Well, the ex-Harvard oarsmen, Stillman and Higgins, have just confessed to witnessing Finley Sparks fall off the Eliot Bridge, but they claim they weren't responsible for it."

"What? How did that happen?"

"They claim that Finley was planning to jump off the bridge freely, as part of a dare. They even livestreamed it on YouTube."

"Wow. What kind of idiots would do that?" Chasen asked.

"It's a Harvard graduation thing, they claim. Usually they jump off Weeks Footbridge, which is closer to campus."

"The final plunge?"

Delaney nodded pensively, then took another sip of his eggnog. "Anyway, Stillman and Higgins claim they tried to rescue Finley when he didn't surface, but they couldn't find him."

"Sounds fishy. Pardon the pun."

"I thought so, too. I locked them up in a cell overnight to let them sleep on it. I imagine they'll be released on bail tomorrow morning as soon as their lawyers get out of bed."

"So, what's still bothering you?"

"I'm not sure," Delaney said. "There are some missing pieces I can't figure out."

"Like what?"

"Well, first of all, Finley fell off the bridge backward, which is definitely odd."

"So, you're thinking maybe somebody pushed him?"

"They must have. The question is, who? Everyone has been accounted for so far."

"True," Sue agreed. "I think you're right, there must be a missing piece somewhere."

"I don't like it," Delaney said. "I also don't like the fact that Sheldon Sparks somehow found out about the arrest, probably from the chief, and now he's going around telling people that the case is closed."

"That guy is a real prizewinner."

"He's a pompous ass," Delaney said. "According to the chief, he's also going around bragging that his wife is pregnant."

"Pregnant? How old is she?"

"About half of his age."

"So, she's a trophy wife."

"I guess."

"Well, it's not like that sort of thing hasn't been done before, especially among the rich and famous. Richard Gere fathered a child at age 70, and so did Tony Randall."

"Yeah, but that's Hollywood. Have you ever known someone who got pregnant with a much older guy, just because he had money?" Delaney asked.

"Hey, some women are attracted to wealth, and they don't mind the age difference," Sue explained.

"Seriously? And you know some of these people?" Delaney asked.

"Sure. Most of my girlfriends would love to have a sugar daddy," she said, trying to hold back a smile.

"So, what are you doing with me?" Delaney asked.

"Oh, you're just my boy toy," Sue teased. "You're not old enough or rich enough to be my sugar daddy. I'll have my fun with you and then toss you on the scrapheap just like all the others."

"That's not a reassuring thought, given your line of work," Delaney said.

Sue Chasen smiled again. It was a good smile, Delaney thought. It spread across her face with total abandon and brought all her different features together. He still couldn't believe that he was dating the chief coroner, but they did mesh rather perfectly together, and her glib sense of humor matched his own.

"What really gets me is that, according to the chief, Sheldon Sparks doesn't seem so broken up about the death of his son anymore," Delaney told her.

"Billionaires are different that way," Chasen said. "People are more like commodities to them. Lose one, gain another."

"I suppose so," Delaney said. "But even your own kid? I mean, that's pretty cold."

"Never underestimate the power of a young woman."

"Meaning?"

"Meaning, it's time to refill our drinks," Sue laughed.

As he listened to the sound of the blender, whipping up another round of eggnogs, Delaney began to replay the final night of Finley's life in his mind again, searching for something he'd overlooked.

"Hey, speaking of women, remember that tattoo you found on Finley's body during the autopsy?" he called out.

"You mean the little owl on his arm? What about it?"

"Well, as it turns out, it wasn't a fraternity insignia after all, but something that might be connected to a mysterious girlfriend."

"Ooh, tell me more." Sue handed him a fresh glass of spiked eggnog, then sat back onto the sofa and slung her legs onto Delaney's lap. "Was her name Athena?"

"What? How did you know?"

"Athena was the Greek goddess of wisdom. Her symbol was the owl."

"Sure, I knew that," Delaney said.

"Of course, an owl can also represent imminent death."

"Now you're joking."

Chasen just shook her head and smiled, sipping her eggnog.

"Okay, how do you know all of this stuff?" Delaney asked. "You don't seem like one of those women who is into astrology."

"Maybe I'm multifaceted, like a diamond," she teased.

"Hmm," Delaney said. "I think we may be getting a little off track here."

"On the contrary, detective," she said. "You need to get in the romantic mood of the victim, who was perhaps madly in love with this mysterious woman."

"Okay, so now we're role-playing?"

"Sure. Let's pretend that you're secretly in love with me, but for some reason you can't tell anyone about our relationship or reveal my name. All you can do is get a secret tattoo in order to express your undying devotion to me."

"Okay," Delaney said, smiling at the obvious parallels to their own relationship.

"So, who am I?" she asked.

"Hmm, I'm not sure. But just so we're clear here, I'm not getting a tattoo."

Chasen rolled her eyes. "Concentrate, detective! What sort of woman am I?"

Delaney shrugged. "Well, you're obviously someone that Stillman and Higgins knew, but Finley couldn't tell them about."

"Yes, but why?"

"Well, either you're embarrassingly ugly . . ."

Chasen frowned and kicked him in the leg. "Or?"

Delaney put down his drink, then stared at her with an excited look. "You're married."

"Bingo!" she exclaimed, kicking him lightly again, this time in the shoulder. Stunned by the revelation and the force of her kick, Delaney fell lazily backward onto the sofa cushions. He lay there for a second, thinking.

"Oops, sorry," Sue laughed, giving him a hand up.

"No, that's brilliant!" he said, with a look of excitement on his face. "I think you might be onto something."

"I am?"

"Yes!" Delaney said, giving her a short and sudden kiss.

"Oh, I like this detective game!" she said. "Let's play more."

"Okay, listen to this. Marsh and I found a strand of hair on Finley's pillow, belonging to Athena Sparks. So, what if—"

"—she was the mysterious girlfriend?"

"Exactly," Delaney said. "But if you were the wife of Sheldon Sparks, what would you be thinking, getting pregnant with him while you are sleeping with his son behind his back?"

"Well, either the son is a hottie, or he's got something else I want."

"You've seen Finley on a slab. I think we can rule out the first motive."

Chasen nodded, grabbing some more rum from the table and pouring it into their drinks.

"So that leaves money . . ." Delaney said.

"Money is part of the equation," she agreed. She stirred her eggnog with her finger, then held it to her lips, tasting to see if the drink was strong enough. "But there may be more to this than meets the eye," she added.

"Like what?" Delaney asked.

"What if Athena Sparks wanted to have a child of her own, but the old goat wasn't up for the job?"

"So, she slept with Finley to get pregnant? That's crazy. Why would she then stick around with Sheldon?"

"Maybe there's some sort of prenup involved."

"I don't know," Delaney said, mulling it over. "It does fit her profile, I suppose. According to Ed Masterson, Athena was a free spirit when it came to relationships. Still, you'd think Sheldon Sparks would be on the lookout for that sort of thing, especially right under his own roof."

"Then again, the last person he'd suspect would be his own son."

"True," Delaney said. "But it still doesn't make complete sense. After all, when the baby was born, the genes would reveal all, including her guilt. Right?"

"But why would anyone check?" Sue pointed out. "And even if they did, the genes might not give him away."

"How so?" Delaney said.

"A son inherits the Y chromosome from his father's DNA, so Finley's child might still appear to be Sheldon's."

"So, Athena Sparks might be off the hook."

"Not only that, but she and her baby would stand to inherit Sheldon's fortune when the old man dies."

"And with Finley dead now, she might get it all."

"Lucky lady," Chasen smiled.

"Unless it's more than just luck," Delaney replied.

· 19 ·

A Lovely Little Theory

"So, if I correctly understand everything you've just told me, Athena Sparks is our new prime suspect?" Joe Martinoli asked. There was a flatness in his voice that barely concealed his annoyance.

"I know it sounds crazy, but it's the only thing that fits," Delaney replied. His partner, Marsh McDonald, gave a tentative nod of agreement.

"Well, it's a lovely little theory. Can you prove it?" the police chief asked.

Delaney nodded. "That's the hard part."

"Yes, that's always the hard part," Martinoli scoffed. "And before you go any further down this new rabbit hole, you'd better fetch me some solid proof. Otherwise, I'll get eaten alive by Sheldon's attorney—and I don't need to see any more lawyers this week."

The chief was referring to the attorney for Brant Stillman and Kyle Higgins, who had waltzed into the state police barracks earlier that day and left soon after with her two clients in tow. The two ex-Harvard oarsmen had quickly regained their sense of smugness as they left the station, confident that there was nowhere near enough evidence to charge them.

"It would help if we could get a copy of Athena's phone records," Marsh interjected.

"And a copy of her prenup agreement with Sheldon," Delaney added.

"Sure thing," Martinoli laughed. "No doubt Sheldon will hand that right over to me. Why don't I just ask him for it during his charity dinner and motorcycle auction this weekend?"

The chief tossed an invitation card across his desk like a frisbee. It slid off the edge and landed at Delaney's feet.

"He might, if he thought his wife was messing around with his son," Marsh persisted.

"Maybe, maybe not. And if we're wrong, then what? We've just ignited a powder keg."

"We'd also be showing our hand to her," Delaney admitted, picking up the invitation card and looking it over. "If she is guilty, Athena Sparks would quickly cover her tracks before we could get to them."

"Well, it sounds like you two are skunked," Martinoli said. "Maybe I should give this case to someone else."

"No," Delaney said, knowing his boss was just testing him. "I think we need to get back into the Sparkses' residence."

"Why? What are you hoping to find that you didn't see the first time?"

"Finley's laptop," Marsh said.

"And who knows what else. Drugs, maybe," Delaney added.

"No probable cause, no warrant; no warrant, no search," Martinoli said.

"Maybe Sheldon would just let us in," Delaney smiled. "On unofficial business."

He held up the invitation card and placed it back on the chief's desk.

Martinoli frowned. "That invite is for me," he said.

"Yes, but aren't you allowed a plus one?" Delaney said.

"No way. I'm not taking either one of you as my date," Martinoli said, laughing. "Besides, I don't think you guys are very popular with Sheldon Sparks right now."

"I wasn't suggesting myself or Marsh," Delaney said. "However, I do know an attractive young woman who has a passion for motorcycles. I'm sure that Sparks would love to show her his collection. And she'd make a charming dinner companion for you."

"I'm not sure I like the sound of that," Martinoli grumbled. "It's highly irregular, to say the least."

"Agreed," Delaney said, smiling back at his boss. The chief picked up the invitation again and turned it around and around in his hands.

"I don't know," Martinoli said. "If I were to even consider this, who would be my date?"

* * * * *

"Let me get this straight. You want me to charm the pants off Sheldon Sparks, get him to give me a tour of his house, then somehow sneak off and find Finley's laptop?" Sue Chasen said.

"That's more or less the shape of it," Delaney replied.

"Sounds very James Bond," Chasen said.

Her voice sounded echoey over the phone, as if on speaker.

"I knew you'd like it."

"I didn't say I liked it, but I'm certainly flattered that you think I'm capable of pulling it off."

There was a brief pause on the other end of the line. Then Delaney heard something that sounded a lot like a bullet being dropped into a metal dish.

"Are you in the middle of dissecting a corpse?" Delaney asked.

"How could you tell?" Sue Chasen answered, cheerfully. "Some gang member was just shot up over on Embankment Road. Nineteen bullet wounds at last count."

"I can call you back," Delaney offered.

"Oh, that's okay, I'm nearly done. I just have to examine the last entry wound near this guy's liver and then sew him up so that he doesn't look like he's been through a woodchipper."

Delaney felt his stomach invert.

"I really didn't need to know that level of detail," he said.

"But I thought we were sharing our work lives now," Sue teased. "Besides, it's nothing you haven't seen before. We met over a corpse, remember?"

"How could I forget?" Delaney said.

Of course, it was one thing to see a dead body and another to visualize it being dissected. But he couldn't explain that to her, any more than he could explain what it was like to see a person get killed.

"So, when do I go undercover?" Sue asked.

"Never mind," Delaney said. "It's a crazy idea and I shouldn't have asked."

"Relax. I'm happy to join the team. Do I get to carry a firearm?"

"No."

"How about a scalpel, hidden in my purse?"

"No."

"C'mon. Not even a tiny little ice pick?"

"You'll wear a Bluetooth, and Marsh and I will communicate with you via cellphone in case you come across something or someone you can't handle."

"Fine, have the chief pick me up at 6 p.m."

*****

Marsh and Delaney were sitting in the front seat of a Verizon cargo van, barely concealed behind a row of arborvitaes that surrounded the Sparks' residence. Luckily, it was already dark at 6:30 p.m., and almost every room in the house was lit. Marsh could easily make out the guests entering the house through a pair of night vision binoculars.

"Wow, is that your girlfriend with the chief?" Marsh asked. "She's pretty hot."

"What? Give me those," Delaney said, tearing the binoculars out of his partner's hands.

He almost didn't recognize Sue, who was clad in a fur coat and a long black dress. She'd even styled her hair differently. Suddenly Delaney felt uncomfortable, like he'd just sent a fly into a spider's web. What they were doing was highly illegal, but Delaney felt it was worth the risk. He'd done this sort of thing only once before, in order to catch a real creep who'd kidnapped a kid.

"By the way, what if we get caught?" Marsh said, as if reading his mind.

"We'll get fired," Delaney said. "And the chief will disavow any involvement with our scheme. Sound check test," he whispered through his cellphone. "Sue, hold up your right hand if you can hear me."

Chasen gave a short wave before she disappeared into the house, remembering not to turn around.

*****

Inside, a live jazz trio was playing a medley of Cole Porter tunes, switching from one song to the next without finishing each composition. The open living area was packed with partygoers, and only the saxophone was loud enough to compete with the dull roar of human voices. A few people were dancing in a living room with vaulted ceilings, while most hovered around a circular table filled with fancy hors d'oeuvres.

Sue felt Sheldon Sparks approach before she saw him, moving toward her like a dark cloud.

"Hello, Joe," he boomed, addressing the police chief like an old friend. The two men briefly shook hands.

"Have we met before?" he asked her, in a jovial tone.

"I don't think so," Chasen lied.

"Susan is an emergency room doctor," Joe Martinoli interjected.

"Really?"

"I'm actually much more interested in motorcycles," she offered. "I hear you have a few for sale."

"I do indeed. Do you ride?"

"I have a Ducati monster," she replied.

She lifted a glass of champagne offered to her from a passing server, while Joe Martinoli wandered over toward the food table.

"Which model?" Sparks inquired.

"The 900 M."

"Impressive."

"It gets me around town," she said, surveying the rest of the party as she sipped her champagne.

She could feel Sparks studying her, trying to decide if he liked what he saw. Luckily, she'd put him off guard enough that he didn't seem to recognize her from the first time they'd met, dressed in a white lab coat and latex gloves, presiding over his son's corpse.

"Do you always wear a Bluetooth to parties?" he asked.

"Only when I'm on call," she explained. "I'm a busy woman."

"Well then, let me show you around," he said, taking her by the arm.

They left Joe Martinoli at the buffet table, stabbing at a plate of cooked shrimp with a toothpick.

At the top of the open staircase on the second floor, Sheldon Sparks stopped to let Sue admire the view below. An elaborate glass and wire sculpture hung from the vaulted ceiling, resembling the wake of a rowing shell. There were a few other pieces of noteworthy artwork scattered about the room, including a small Picasso that Sparks pointed out near the entryway.

"Isn't that a bit risky?" Sue asked. "I mean, putting an expensive piece of art like that right near your front door?"

"Hidden in plain sight," Sparks explained. "Any thief would walk right by it, thinking that anything valuable wouldn't be there."

Sue mulled this over, as she turned her attention to the partygoers below. Suddenly she caught the eye of a young blonde, who was staring back at her intensely.

"What's with the woman in the green silk dress?" she asked.

"Oh, don't mind her; she's just my wife."

"Okay," she laughed.

They proceeded toward the inner rooms of the second floor. Still holding onto her arm, Sheldon nearly dragged her into his study. It was a dark, cavernous room swathed in wall-to-wall red carpeting and wood paneling. She detected a faint odor of tobacco. A long wooden Harvard oar hung above a large desk.

"This is my command center," her host said proudly.

The walls were adorned with various business awards and photos of Sheldon standing beside other famous billionaires, including Warren Buffet and Richard Branson. Sue gave the obligatory *oohs* and *aahs*, pretending to admire everything while she scanned the room for nooks and crannies that might hold a laptop.

Sheldon hovered over her shoulder as she circled the room. She could smell the whiskey on his breath, intermingled with a bad case of halitosis. Suddenly she felt herself fighting back a case of nausea.

"What's in that room, across the hall?" she asked, pivoting back toward the door. Before Sheldon could answer, she made an enthusiastic exit.

Athena's art studio was the polar opposite of Sheldon's study, with ivory walls and multiple sources of natural and artificial light. Sue immediately felt more comfortable, knowing that Delaney and Marsh could see her through the front windows. The large canvases contained abstract swaths of color intersecting with one another, combining to produce other colors and shapes. Some of it had mildly sexual overtones in the style of Georgia O'Keeffe.

"That one always reminds me of a naked body," Sheldon ventured, pointing at a work in progress set up on an easel. "What do you think?"

"Hmmm. I don't quite see it," she said, trying not to grin knowing that Delaney and Marsh were listening to every word of their conversation.

"Well, given your line of work, I imagine that you are well-versed in human anatomy," Sparks said, resting his hand on her shoulder again.

"Intimately," she said, trying not to laugh at his predictability. In medical school, she and her colleagues had mastered all the morbid jokes that involved sexual innuendo, and Sheldon's pickup line was about as clichéd as they came.

Suddenly a woman's voice called out from the stairs, beckoning him below.

"Sounds like mommy is calling," Sue Chasen teased.

"I'd better get back to the other guests," Sheldon muttered. "We can see the bikes later."

"Of course," she said. "Do you mind if I use the powder room before I rejoin the party?"

He pointed her toward a door down the hallway as he made a hasty exit in the opposite direction. When he'd disappeared down the stairs, she took the cellphone carefully out of her purse.

"Okay, where do I find this thing?" she whispered.

"Think about where you'd hide the laptop of someone you were having an affair with," Delaney said.

"I don't have any experience with that," she chided the detective. "Do you?"

"Be serious. We don't have much time here."

"You be serious," she snapped back.

"Okay, just relax." Delaney said.

Sue walked quickly around Athena's art studio, checking the drawers of a flat file storage cabinet. They were filled with artwork, paper, pencils, and paint. Then she tried a closet. The shelves held various cleaning supplies and solvents. Another dead end. She looked around the room again, scanning the completed paintings that hung on the walls.

Only one of them wasn't an abstract study, a recent portrait of Finley. It was encased in an oversized, black frame. On a hunch, she lifted it off the picture mount. It was exceptionally heavy. She laid it down on the floor and ran her fingers along the brown paper backing. Something was definitely inside.

* * * * *

"You heard that the flasher struck again?" Marsh said to Delaney, just to pass the time.

"What? The guy on the Charles River?"

"Yep."

"That's impossible," Delaney said.

He'd spoken with Raymond St. James over a month ago and laid down the law to both him and his parents. Rather than face police charges, Delaney had persuaded the parents to ship their son off to a counseling center in Western Massachusetts. He'd kept the whole thing quiet since he'd grown up with St. James and knew that he was essentially harmless. If he went to prison, he'd get eaten alive.

"Well, he's struck again," Marsh said.

"That's weird," Delaney said.

"Yeah, but at least this time the girl who reported him was a runner, not a rower, and she was able to get a better look at him. Here's the sketch."

Marsh showed him the artist's rendering on his cellphone. The guy had a familiar face, but Delaney couldn't quite place it. Then Sue's voice came over the speaker phone.

"I've got it! What do I do now?"

"What kind of laptop is it?" Marsh asked.

"Mac."

"Okay. Slide the active USB drive into the port, then turn it on," Marsh instructed.

"What if I need a password?" she asked.

"That doesn't matter. The USB drive will copy the files anyway."

Delaney and Marsh could hear the familiar, F-sharp major chime as the MacBook powered up.

"I'm going to take a crack at the password, just for kicks," Sue Chasen said. "A-T-H-E-N-A," she said out loud, typing in the six letters.

"Isn't that a bit obvious?" Delaney said.

"I'm in!" Sue said triumphantly. "Even the screen saver is a picture of you-know-who, lying on a beach somewhere."

"Very nice. I'm sure," Delaney said. "Have all the files finished loading into the USB drive?"

"Not yet . . . oh crap!" he heard Chasen swear.

"What?"

Delaney heard her slam the laptop closed. Then he heard another woman's voice in the distance.

"What the hell do you think you're doing?" the voice said.

Sue looked up and saw Athena Sparks, standing in the doorway.

· 20 ·

A Shadow in the Night

"*I* could ask you the same question," Sue Chasen replied, tapping the top of Finley's computer with her right hand as she palmed the USB drive into her left. "Withholding evidence is a serious crime."

Her bold repartee had the desired effect. Athena Sparks opened her mouth to speak, then checked herself, tilting her head to one side as if to reconsider.

"I couldn't have people find out certain things," she said finally.

"Like your affair with Finley?"

Athena closed the door behind her, then came and sat down on the corner of the bed.

"So, you found the emails?" she asked.

Sue nodded, continuing forward with her risky gambit. She was in it this far and to back out now might prove difficult, if not dangerous.

Athena fell silent again. Suddenly, she looked like she was about to cry.

"You must be devastated by all of this," Sue offered, softening her tone. "Clearly you two really cared for each other."

"Neither one of us wanted a relationship," the younger woman sighed. "When I first married Sheldon, Finley despised me. After all, we were closer in age than Sheldon and me, and I clearly wasn't going to be any kind of mother figure to him. Eventually he accepted me, and we became more like brother and sister. And then, well . . . you know the rest."

"When did things get intimate?" Sue asked.

"Only recently, over the past few months. We essentially bonded over the fact that both of us were under Sheldon's thumb."

"I can understand how that might happen," Sue replied. "But don't you think you should explain all of this directly to the police? I'm pretty sure they're looking at you as a prime suspect."

"What? That's crazy! Wait, aren't you a police officer?"

Sue shook her head. "Sorry, I never properly introduced myself. I'm Sue Chasen. I'm the chief coroner. I'm just helping out the police as a medical consultant."

"Oh," Athena said, taking this in. "But why would they think that I killed Finley?"

Sue tilted her head and suppressed a smile. She was starting to like this interrogation game.

"Well, you two got together on the night of his death, didn't you?"

"Yes, we met in Harvard Square. I tried to talk him out of the whole bridge-jumping stunt he'd gotten dragged into."

"You weren't with him on the bridge?"

She shook her head. "I wish I was. I might have prevented this whole thing from happening. Instead, I had to deal with a crazy, threatening phone call from my ex."

"You mean Finley's old rowing coach?"

Athena nodded. "Ed Masterson."

"What did he want?"

"The usual nonsense. He basically never accepted the fact that we broke up a few years ago. He's been stalking and harassing me on and off for months."

"Have you reported that to the police?"

Athena shook her head.

"Why not?"

"It's complicated. After all, we were engaged to be married."

"Sounds pretty straightforward to me. The guy is a creep."

"Oh, it's much worse than that," Athena said. "I'm pretty sure he's a high-functioning psychopath."

"Seriously? Why do you say that?"

"Well, I'm getting my PhD in psych, and I study this sort of thing—although a lot of good it's done me in choosing men. I actually met Ed when he attended a class that I was leading a section in at Harvard called abnormal psych."

"How ironic," Sue remarked.

Athena nodded in agreement.

"He was super charming at first, and good-looking in a rugged, athletic sort of way. Plus, he was genuinely smart. I mean, the papers he wrote for class were a little bizarre, but some of them were on the verge of brilliant. Long story short, I got curious about him."

"And you crossed the teacher–student boundary?"

Athena shrugged. "More like, I jumped over it. Still, it's not like he was an undergraduate or anything. He's a few years older than I am."

"Okay, no judgment. I've done that sort of thing myself before. And then?"

"Well, we quickly got wrapped up in each other's lives. It was amazing for about eight months. I mean, I really thought that he was 'the one.' And then, things just started to get weird."

"Explain?"

"As soon as we got engaged, things changed. He wanted to know every move I made—right down to where I was going to get my next cup of coffee. He'd text me constantly, asking where I was and what I was doing. I've always been pretty independent, so that sort of thing didn't sit well with me."

"I know the type," Sue agreed, knowing that Sean Delaney was still listening. "Some guys think they own you, just because you share a glass of eggnog with them."

"He was also super manipulative, and not just with me."

"How so?"

"He was obsessed with rowing and winning at all costs, even if it meant compromising the mental health and integrity of his team. One day, he told me that he'd figured out a way to get the guys to row harder by pitting them against one another psychologically. When I brought up the ethical issues of using this strategy, he just shrugged it off and claimed that everyone did it."

"What sort of thing are we talking about here?" Sue asked. "I mean, a lot of coaches can be borderline sadistic."

"This was different. It was much more calculated in a way that made him look removed from it all. According to Finley, he used him as his mouthpiece, feeding him all sorts of confidential information about his teammates and telling him how to use it against them."

"Hmm. That does sound pretty twisted."

Athena nodded. "It wasn't until recently that I learned all the details. Finley gradually opened up to me after I began to share my own troubled past with Ed."

"Did Finley feel bad about his role with the team?"

"Of course. Everyone on his crew hated him, and he desperately wanted to come clean. He told his dad, of course, and Sheldon got Masterson fired from Harvard, but he never told his boatmates. I think he was planning to do it on the night we were supposed to meet, the night he—"

Athena stopped talking and fought back a few tears.

"So do you think he jumped?" Sue said, handing her a Kleenex.

"No way. He was pushed, and I'm pretty sure that Masterson did it."

"Why do you say that?"

"Somehow Ed had figured out that Finley and I were having an affair. He got me to admit it that night. Then he started yelling over the phone and told me he was going to do something about it."

"What? Athena, this is crazy! You have to tell the police!"

Suddenly the bedroom door flew wide open.

"Tell them what?" Sheldon Sparks boomed.

* * * * *

Sean Delaney didn't need the night vision binoculars to observe Sue Chasen through the studio window on the second floor. His long-range vision was excellent, and there was enough light in the room to see her clearly. But when the silhouette of another woman had entered the room, he reached over to take the glasses from Marsh, who'd been using them to randomly scan the woods around the property.

"Wait, I think I saw something," Marsh whispered.

"Where?" Delaney asked.

"Over there, near the woodpile. It looked pretty big."

"Probably just a deer," Delaney said. "The woods out here are loaded with them."

"Technically speaking, deer aren't nocturnal," Marsh retorted. "They are crepuscular."

"Whatever, Marsh. Just give me the damn glasses," Delaney said. "You should be paying more attention to what's happening *inside* the house. Have you been listening to this conversation? Sue's amazing."

"Yes, Chasen is doing pretty well, I guess."

"Pretty well? She's knocking it out of the park, Marsh. I hope you're recording all of this."

"I am, but I'm not sure why. After all, none of it will be admissible in court."

"I don't care, it's still worth having."

The two kept listening to the conversation.

"Now that was a low blow," Delaney remarked when Sue made the comment about eggnog.

"How so?" Marsh said.

"Never mind," Delaney replied. "I can't believe that we got taken in by Masterson."

"Confirmation bias," Marsh quipped.

"What?"

"It's when you interpret evidence based on a preconceived notion of what happened—"

"I know what confirmation bias is, Marsh," Delaney groaned. "Besides, at that point we never suspected Athena Sparks was so involved."

"No, but we were willing to believe Masterson's story that she was a sex-crazed drug addict and a gold digger to boot."

Delaney said nothing. Marsh had a point.

"Hey, boss, there it is again!" Marsh said. "Look!"

Marsh pointed toward the woodpile that lay on the far side of the driveway, just beyond the reach of the outdoor floodlights. Delaney didn't need night vision glasses to see the tall bulky figure stand up and scurry toward the backyard, dressed in a lumberjack coat.

"Call it in on the radio, now!" he barked at Marsh. "I'll find a way to warn the chief and Sue. Who knows what this guy is up to, but he looks suspicious."

"Do you think it might be one of the catering guys?" Marsh said. "Out having a smoke?"

"I doubt it," Delaney said. "By the way, have you ever used your service revolver?"

"I was the top cadet at the firing range."

"This isn't the firing range, Marsh, and we're not hunting deer. You take the front entrance; I'll take the back."

The two detectives piled out of the van and ran toward the house.

* * * * *

Sheldon Sparks stood in the doorway, beer bottle in hand, waiting for an answer to his question.

"Oh, hi, Sheldy. We're just having a little chat," Athena said.

"I can see that, but what do you have to tell the police?" he said.

Athena sighed. "Oh, it's just that jerk, Ed Masterson. I was just telling Sue that he'd been bothering me again, and she advised me to go to the police."

"You never told *me* that!" Sheldon barked. "How long has this been going on?"

"Sorry to interrupt," Sue said, holding up her hand as she listened to Delaney through her Bluetooth. "But I think you folks may have a prowler on the premises."

"What?" Sheldon Sparks said, becoming even more confused and agitated. "What the hell is going on here?"

Sue stood up and made for the doorway. "Sorry, but right now I need to go downstairs. Sergeant Delaney will be here any moment, and I'm sure he'll explain everything to you."

She sure hoped he could. Otherwise, they might all be in a bit of a tight spot.

* * * * *

Delaney and Marsh had already circled the house twice with flashlights when Chief Martinoli came out the front door. Sheldon Sparks was right behind him.

"What's the situation, Sergeant?" the chief said.

"Someone called in a possible breaking and entering," Delaney lied.

"Did you try the outbuilding?" Sparks suggested. "He's probably after my motorcycle collection!"

"Let's go, Marsh," Delaney said. "Mr. Sparks, I would advise you to stay in the house with your party guests and make sure all the doors and windows are locked."

"No way. Besides, you'll need the access code."

"Marsh, you stay with the guests," Martinoli instructed. "Delaney, lead the way."

As they approached the outbuilding, the trio could barely make out a small light turned on in the studio apartment.

"That's Finley's old room," Sheldon whispered. "What's he doing in there?"

"More important," Delaney said. "How did he get in without setting off the alarm?"

"There's only one way in, and one way out," Sheldon said, punching in the access code.

"What's the plan, boss?" Delaney said to the chief.

"It's quite simple. Go in there and check it out."

Several minutes later, Delaney emerged, leading a handcuffed man in front of him. As they walked past the police chief and Sheldon Sparks, the detective stopped, briefly, and shone the flashlight up into his prisoner's face. The man closed his eyes and averted his gaze from the light, but he was clearly recognizable.

"Ed Masterson!" Sheldon Sparks growled. "Well, I hope you lock him up for good this time!"

Masterson just shook his head silently, as Delaney led him away.

· 21 ·

A Good Lie

"*I* think I need a drink after all that," Chasen said, plopping down into an overstuffed chair. She took a quick look around Delaney's apartment, which looked like a cheap hotel room. It smelled faintly like a gym.

"You certainly deserve one," Delaney said. "Great job tonight."

"Thanks, but I don't think I ever want to do that again. I'll stick to examining people after they've died."

Delaney smiled and poured her a glass of Merlot from a previously opened bottle that he'd failed to recork.

"Sorry, it's all I have," he apologized.

"Desperate times," Sue quipped. "So, what was Ed Masterson doing in the Sparkses' garage tonight?"

"He claims that Athena told him to meet him there, even gave him the access code beforehand."

"Okay, that's weird," she said, trying not to wince after she tasted her wine.

"Well, at least that explains why the alarm didn't go off," Delaney said.

"But why invite someone over during a huge house party?" Sue asked. "Unless you purposely want to have them get caught."

"Maybe that was Athena's plan," Delaney said. "She seemed pretty convincing tonight in her portrayal of Masterson as an abusive ex-boyfriend. Setting him up could've been payback."

"It was definitely a good performance," Sue agreed.

"So, you don't believe her?"

She shrugged. "What else did Masterson say, when you got him back to the station?"

"He still maintains that he's innocent of any wrongdoing, both tonight and on the Charles River."

"And you believe him?" Sue asked.

Delaney shrugged and took another sip of wine.

"He did confess to an off-again, on-again relationship with Athena, even after she married Sheldon Sparks, but when I mentioned her recent allegations about him, he went ballistic. He seemed genuinely surprised, confused, and pissed-off."

"So, either Masterson is a great liar, or he's a total chump who just got played by his ex."

Delaney nodded. "You were in the same room as Athena. What did you think of her?"

"Well, she certainly had me on her side for a while, but she doesn't strike me as the victim type—way too smart."

"Smart women can still be victims," Delaney countered.

"Certainly," Sue agreed. "Sometimes they're even made to drink day-old wine."

"Hey, nobody's forcing you," Delaney laughed.

Sue gave a mock grimace as she stared down at her abandoned Merlot, as if weighing the pros and cons of taking another sip.

"Okay, so what's your take, detective?" she asked. "Is Athena Sparks lying, or is she telling the truth? After all, you and Marsh were listening in to most of our conversation over Bluetooth."

"A good lie always has some element of truth to it," Delaney mused. He was starting to feel the liberating effects of the alcohol.

"That's very philosophical of you, but cut to the chase. What part of her story is true and what part is not?"

"Ah, yes. Now we come to the real detective work."

"Why not just get them in the same room together and grill them?" Sue suggested.

"Great idea, but it's a little more complicated than that. Remember, Athena Sparks isn't guilty of anything yet, and she knows it. For that matter, neither is Ed Masterson, aside from a possible breaking and entering charge. We can't omit the possibility that they might have been working together, at least initially, so I need to keep them both guessing about what we know and play them off each other."

"So, what do we do now?" Sue asked, with a tone of frustration edging into her voice. She was beginning to get annoyed by the way Delaney seemed to be enjoying himself, using her as a foil for his own problem-solving process. That, and the fact that she was still sober.

"Basically, we need more information. There are still a lot of unanswered questions that would help us decide our next course of action,"

Delaney said. "Like whose child is Athena Sparks carrying, and how might that tie into a motive for murder?"

"And now we have three possibilities for the paternity, not just two," Sue pointed out.

Delaney nodded, refilling his wine glass. Suddenly he smiled, realizing how much he enjoyed his repartee with Sue. She'd become much more of a partner to him than Marsh McDonald ever had been.

"It might be helpful if we could gain access to Athena and Sheldon Sparks's medical records," he said. "I'll be willing to bet that they visited a fertility clinic somewhere along the line. There could be some clues hidden among all the paperwork."

"Obtaining that would be totally illegal, but there might be a better source of information," Sue suggested.

"Where?" Delaney asked.

"Not where, but who. Sheldon's ex-wife, Irene—the one who showed up for Finley's autopsy. I bet she knows everything there is to know about Sheldon's medical history, including his virility or lack thereof."

"Great idea," Delaney said. "I owe you a dinner *and* a decent bottle of wine."

"That's for sure," Sue laughed, reaching over and bravely draining her glass.

"One thing is certain—Athena Sparks was quite the femme fatale," she continued. "And quite possibly a criminal mastermind."

"How so?" Delaney asked.

"Well, when you step back and think about it, she could've orchestrated this whole thing from the start, using all three men as her pawns."

"It's definitely an interesting theory," Delaney said. "But as the chief would say, with no proof, I can't make something like that stick. In court, it might easily come off as conjecture. Any good lawyer would tear it apart."

"It's not all conjecture," Sue protested. "Remember, according to Masterson, Athena was polyamorous, so she'd have no problem with that part of the equation."

"You mean like 'any old port in a storm?'" Delaney teased.

"Charming," Chasen said. "Talk about a typical male response."

"Guilty as charged."

"What I meant was, Athena might have purposefully slept with all three men to get exactly what she wanted—money, prestige, and a baby to boot. And then she leaves the crew coach holding the bag."

"That's quite a trifecta," Delaney said. "But again, we need proof."

They mulled it over a bit, sipping their wine. Delaney's cellphone rang. "State Police Barracks" popped up on the caller ID. He put the call on speaker after he answered it.

"What is it, Marsh? It's almost midnight, and I'm trying to get some sleep," Delaney said, winking at Chasen.

"Sorry, boss, but DeFavio and I are still combing through those downloads from Finley's computer. I think there's something you need to see."

"Okay, but can't it wait until morning?"

"I guess," Marsh replied, sounding disappointed.

"Okay, okay. What is it?"

"Well, remember that video of Finley jumping off the bridge? The one we thought his teammates took?"

"And later claimed they deleted?"

"Yeah, well, it looks like it was uploaded onto Finley's Facebook page from his laptop, after the fact. It must have been done by Athena Sparks, unless Finley can code from the grave."

"Good work, Marsh. See you bright and early."

"So, what does that mean?" Sue asked.

"It means we can finally bring Athena Sparks in for questioning."

· 22 ·

Coup de Grace

$\mathscr{D}$etective Anthony DeFavio squinted at the laptop he was examining, clicking through several different screens as he worked the eraser end of a pencil into his left ear.

"Okay, that's gross, Anthony," Linda Matthews said.

"What?" DeFavio said.

"You're disgusting," the dispatch officer reiterated.

"Oh relax, Linda," DeFavio said. "I have to watch you put ChapStick on your lips every ten minutes. So, what if I take a little wax out of my ear every now and then? Same difference."

"It's not really the same, Anthony," Marsh McDonald chimed in. "Unless you are thinking of using earwax as ChapStick?"

"Hmm . . . interesting thought," DeFavio said, as if he were considering the idea.

"Oh my god," Matthews groaned. "Seriously? I need a raise if I'm going to continue to work around you two knuckleheads."

Delaney entered the front door in time to catch her last comment.

"Are Laurel and Hardy at it again?" he asked.

"Hey, boss, I thought you told us to be here 'bright and early,'" Marsh asked.

"I did," Delaney responded. "But I never said I'd be in early, did I?"

"Nice one," DeFavio snorted.

"You guys both look like hell," Delaney added. "Did you sleep here last night?"

Marsh and DeFavio looked at each other sheepishly.

"Where did you sleep?" DeFavio retorted. "Your place or hers?"

"None of your damn business," Delaney said.

"You know, it must be kind of weird, dating a coroner," DeFavio said. "I mean, think about it."

He looked over at Marsh, lifting his eyebrows.

"I have a better idea—don't," Delaney said. "Why don't you tell me what you found on Finley Sparks's laptop?"

"Oh, there were lots of goodies on here," DeFavio said, eagerly pawing at the keyboard. "Other than the video that Marsh already told you about, the best part of the treasure trove was Finley's text messages."

"They were recorded on his laptop?"

DeFavio nodded. "Total rookie mistake, synching them up to his Mac. Unless, of course, he did it on purpose."

"So, whom was he texting with on the night he died?" Delaney asked.

"Bit of a surprise there. See for yourself," he said, spinning the computer around.

"I'll be damned," Delaney said, looking at the texts. "Well, this certainly changes things a little."

"I'd say so," DeFavio agreed. "Talk about an Oedipus complex."

"Who's got an Oedipus complex?" Chief Joe Martinoli asked, emerging from his office with a Dunkin' Donuts coffee in one hand and a half-eaten cruller in the other.

"Probably every guy in this room," Linda Matthews quipped.

"Very funny, Linda," Martinoli said. "Okay, team. Big day, right? Where are we?"

"Well, Mr. and Mrs. Sparks should be arriving any minute now," Delaney said. "The crew coach spent the night here with us."

"He's not a happy camper," DeFavio added.

"I wouldn't be either, if I'd been picked up three times on suspicion of murder," Marsh pointed out.

"So, what's the plan of attack?" the chief asked.

"Marsh will take one last crack at Masterson, just to make sure every detail of his story checks out. You and I can handle Sheldon and Athena Sparks."

"Don't you think we should split everyone up and talk to them separately?"

Delaney shook his head.

"My instinct is to put them together in the same room and see what happens."

"That sounds like the recipe for a barroom brawl," the chief said.

"I was thinking more in terms of a bullfight," Delaney said. "And to do that, we need to provoke the bull."

As if on cue, Sheldon Sparks came barging through the front door with Athena Sparks following closely at his heels. They were wearing their matching shearling coats, as if they were arriving for a fashion shoot instead of an interrogation.

"Thanks for coming in," Joe Martinoli said, stepping forward to shake Sheldon's hand.

"What's this all about, Joe?" he said. "And why do you need to talk to my wife?" He scanned the room with a jaundiced eye, barely acknowledging Delaney and Marsh.

"Everything's fine, Sheldon, we just need to clear up a few last things. Come on into the conference room and tell Detective Delaney what you want in your coffee."

Delaney exchanged a sharp look with his boss. As he dutifully fetched two cups, he overheard Martinoli exchange pleasantries with the Sparkses.

"How's the baby coming along? What is it now, six months?"

"Eight, actually," Athena corrected.

"She's barely showing," Sheldon said. "But the bun is definitely about to pop out of the oven."

"Such a romantic," his wife replied. Delaney tried to hand her a coffee, but she gave him a dismissive wave.

"So, Mr. Sparks, you got a vasectomy in 2005, correct?" he asked.

"What does that have to do with anything?" Sheldon barked, instantly turning red. "And that's privileged information!"

"In a murder investigation, nothing is privileged," Delaney replied. "Your ex-wife Irene told us."

Sparks took a sip of his coffee and frowned, trying to recover his composure. "This is a far cry from Starbucks," he grumbled.

"So, I'm just curious how you and your wife got pregnant," Delaney persisted.

"None of your damn business," he said.

"Now, Sheldon," Joe Martinoli interrupted.

"Now what? If you two read your biology textbooks back in high school, you'd know that a pregnancy can still occur after a vasectomy," Sparks said.

"Unlikely, but true," Delaney said.

He beckoned to Marsh, who was waiting just outside the conference room door.

Marsh escorted Ed Masterson into the room, holding him by the back of the arm. The ex-crew coach was wearing handcuffs, with a defiant, hostile look on his face.

"What's he doing here?" Sparks said. His wife shifted uncomfortably in her chair.

"Relax, Sheldon. Sergeant Delaney just needs to clear up a few details about the night your son died."

"You mean the night he was murdered by this hoodlum?"

Masterson closed his eyes and shook his head.

"Mr. Sparks, you told us that you were at home with your wife that night," Delaney resumed. "Is that correct?"

"Yes, I've told you that already. What the hell is this, Joe? I feel like I'm the one being interrogated here."

"You're not being questioned under caution," the chief clarified. "But if you want a lawyer, we can easily arrange it."

Sheldon Sparks shook his head dismissively. "Of course not."

"Can you confirm that your husband was home, Mrs. Sparks?" Delaney continued.

"What do you mean?" Athena asked.

"It's a simple question. Were you at home with your husband all night?"

She lowered her head as Ed Masterson glared at her, waiting for her response.

"Well, I'm not sure. I had to run some errands at the college early on."

"I take it you mean Harvard University?" Delaney asked. "So, what time did you actually get home?"

"Again, I'm not sure," she said. "Maybe 7 or 8 p.m.?" She glanced over at her husband for help, but Sheldon just shrugged.

"I don't keep track of my wife's exact movements, and she doesn't keep track of mine."

"I beg to differ," Delaney said. "Mrs. Sparks, isn't it true that you met with Finley that night in Harvard Square, where the two of you often met for romantic dates?"

"What?" Sheldon erupted. "This is outrageous! Let's go, honey, we're out of here."

He stood up, but his wife remained seated.

"Yes," Athena finally whispered.

Sheldon sat back down, slack-jawed.

"And isn't it true that you were also having an affair with Ed Masterson at the same time?"

Athena Sparks grew quiet again.

"Yes, she was," Ed Masterson said, answering the question for her.

"So, you were still stringing Ed along, until, somehow, he found out about you and Finley. He called you up and confronted you about it on the night of Finley's death, didn't he?"

Masterson nodded in agreement.

"I think I want a lawyer now," Athena said. "Honey?"

Sheldon Sparks didn't respond. He pursed his lips together in silent contempt.

"So how did you feel about that, Ed?" Delaney said.

"I was pretty damn upset, as you might imagine."

"Enough to push Finley off the Eliot Bridge?"

"No way. I was mad at Athena, not Finley. She kept telling me I was the father of her child."

"So, you felt used?" Delaney asked.

"Exactly. She clearly just wanted to have sex with me to get pregnant. The big man over there apparently couldn't produce."

Sheldon flushed a shade of crimson that nearly matched his Harvard tie. The big muscle above his jaw began to twitch as he tried desperately to control his anger.

"Is this an interview or a group therapy session?" he scoffed.

"Yes, get to the point, detective," Chief Martinoli urged.

"Okay, here's what I think, Mr. Sparks. You already knew that your wife was having an affair with your son's old crew coach, didn't you?" Delaney continued. "You'd been having the two of them tailed for weeks, and you even put a tracking device on Athena's phone. Unfortunately, your son found out about it."

Athena looked over at her husband with her mouth wide open, as if she were too stunned to speak.

"So what?" Sheldon Sparks replied. "When you've been around the block as many times as I have, trust is hard to come by. I mean, a man like me needs some sort of insurance."

"Really?" Athena Sparks said, with a tone of disgust in her voice.

"Yeah, really," Sheldon fired back. "Good thing, too, because you were setting me up like a chump."

"Welcome to the club," Ed Masterson chuckled.

"Okay, okay," Delaney said. "Let's get back to the night in question. And now I *am* placing you under caution, so think carefully before you respond. Mr. Sparks, you knew that Athena was planning to meet Finley at the Eliot Bridge, correct?"

Sheldon hesitated for a second, then shrugged his bearlike shoulders in acquiescence.

"But Athena never made it to the bridge, did she?"

"That's right," Athena said. "I got stuck talking to *him*." She shot an angry look across the table at Ed Masterson.

"So, here's what I think happened," Delaney continued, keeping his focus on Sheldon Sparks. "You showed up at the bridge, expecting to confront your wife about her infidelities, but instead you found Finley all by himself. You got angry with him, and then the two of you got into it."

"No way," Sheldon Sparks said, looking from side to side, and then toward the door. Everyone in the room was now looking at him intently.

"I should tell you that we found traces of Finley's blood on the bridge," Delaney added. "And I bet if we look closer, we're going to find your DNA somewhere . . ."

"I—I didn't mean for anything bad to happen," Sheldon sputtered. "Yes, I found Finley on the bridge. And yes, I did get angry with him. He and his friends were in the middle of some sort of stupid college prank, and he told me to leave him alone. I said 'No.' Then I tried to question him about Athena; he just laughed at me and called me a cuckold."

"Which you are," Ed Masterson muttered, loud enough for everyone to hear.

Sheldon Sparks stopped talking and glowered across the table.

"Go on, tell us the rest of the story, Sheldon," the chief said. "Get it off your chest."

"Well, I guess I completely lost it. I started yelling, and then . . ." Sheldon hesitated for a moment, as his voice cracked.

"And then?" Delaney said.

"I guess I must've cuffed him pretty hard across the head, because he fell backward and flipped over the bridge."

"Oh my god," Athena said. "*You* killed him. You killed your own son!"

Sheldon just sat there and looked at his wife, with a puzzled expression on his face. Then he slumped forward and hid his face in his hands, as if he'd just realized what he'd done. A giant wail came out of him that sounded like a wounded animal.

"Did you hit him with your right or left hand?" Delaney asked.

"What?" Sparks said, in between sobs. "I don't know! Left, I suppose. What difference does it make?"

"Mr. Sparks, I'm going to have to ask you to remove your wedding ring, so that I can test it for samples of your son's DNA."

Sparks didn't respond at first. He was still sobbing pitifully into his hands.

"You may as well hand it over, babe. Our marriage is over anyway," said Athena Sparks. She removed her own wedding ring and slid it across the table like a hockey puck.

"Ma'am, I don't need your ring, just your husband's."

"Well, I sure as hell don't want it anymore."

"Maybe you can pawn it and make a few bucks," Masterson suggested.

"But I don't understand, Sheldon," Chief Martinoli interrupted. "Why didn't you call 911 right then and there?"

"I don't know," Sparks said, lifting his head from his hands. "I guess, at first, I thought he might have survived the fall. I heard shouting under the bridge and then the sound of a motor launch with his teammates in it. I was hoping maybe they'd rescued him."

"But what about afterward? Did you try to call your son to make sure he was okay?"

Sheldon shook his head, trying to wipe the tears from his eyes.

"His phone wasn't taking calls. I did call Bob Rousseau, over at the Harvard police, and he told me to sit tight until the next day."

"When the two of you tried to direct the blame over to Ed Masterson?" Delaney asked.

Sparks offered no response.

"I can't believe you killed your own son," Athena Sparks repeated.

The chief motioned to a few duty officers, who came into the room and began to handcuff Sheldon Sparks. Delaney quietly read him his rights, then removed his wedding ring and put it into a plastic evidence bag.

Ed Masterson sat and watched patiently as Sheldon Sparks was led from the room.

"Can I get out of these now?" he finally asked, holding up his handcuffs.

* * * * *

When the interview was formally over, Delaney excused himself and went to the bathroom. He had a sudden, overwhelming desire to wash his hands and face and be alone for a few minutes, but Marsh followed him.

"Now that was really something," he said.

"Yeah. It was something all right," Delaney said. "Listen, Marsh, good work and all that, but can we talk about the whole thing later, after I've had a little time to decompress?"

"Sure thing, boss," Marsh said.

After Marsh had left him alone, Delaney took out his cellphone and dialed Sue Chasen.

"Sorry I haven't called," he said. "I just got through with the interrogation."

"How'd it go?" she asked, tentatively.

"Pretty intense. We just got Sheldon Sparks for first-degree murder."

"Wow," she said. "I didn't see that one coming."

"Yeah, it's totally weird. I mean, the same guy who insisted that we look for a killer turned out to be the killer himself."

"Hidden in plain sight," Sue said.

"What's that?" Delaney asked.

"Nothing," Sue replied. "Tell me how and why he did it."

"He found out about Athena and Finley and went berserk. He whacked his son over the head."

"I guess that explains the blunt force trauma."

"Yep. And I'm pretty sure that cut on Finley's head you found came from Sheldon's wedding ring, but we'll have to confirm it with the lab."

"So, the wedding ring was the murder weapon?"

"Very likely."

"Well, that's a new one on me," Sue Chasen said.

"Me too," Delaney agreed. "Makes you think twice about getting married."

"Why? Have you been thinking about that lately?"

"No, I'm only saying . . ." Delaney backpedaled.

"Because if you have, then I have another confession to make," Sue said.

"Okay, but do you have to tell me right now?" Delaney asked. "I've heard a few too many confessions today."

"Don't worry, it's nothing serious," Sue reassured him. "I was just going to tell you that I'm not the sort of gal who is into rings, or churches, or any of those things. I mean, we can just go to the courthouse and then have a small gathering afterward."

"Woah. Hold on a sec. How did we go down this detour?" Delaney protested. "I think I need a drink or something before we have this conversation."

"I know just what you need, and I'm right outside to give it to you."

"Now that sounds more promising. You're here at the barracks?"

"Yup. I wanted to be there for you to the end of this craziness."

Delaney walked out into the parking lot and immediately spotted the red Ducati. The motorcycle engine was still running, with its low, throaty growl.

"C'mon. Get on," Sue said, handing him an extra helmet. She was dressed in black jeans and stylish cowboy boots.

"I don't know," Delaney said. "My mother told me never to accept a ride with a stranger. I mean, what do I really know about you?"

"Everything that counts," she said. "But if you really must know, I went to Barnard and finished first in my class."

"Oh, well in that case . . ." Delaney said, clambering onto the back of the bike.

"Where should we go?" she asked.

"Anywhere but here," Delaney said.

"Do I need to stick to the speed limit, Sergeant?"

"Absolutely not. But can we make a quick pit stop at the 7-Eleven at the end of Charles Street, first? There's someone I want you to meet."

"Okay, but that sounds mysterious. I hope you're not thinking I'm going to be a cheap date tonight?"

"Not at all," Delaney said. "This will only take a second. Afterward, I'm thinking we can walk over to the Liberty Hotel in the old jail house and eat at Scampo's. And later, if you like, we can drive over to Wally's and listen to some real jazz."

"That sounds more like it. And where do we finally end up this evening?"

Delaney smiled again. "I think we both know the answer to that question."

Sue smiled back and then lowered the plastic visor of her helmet.

They pulled away from the state police station at Leverett Circle and swung onto Storrow Drive. Delaney felt the sudden adrenaline rush flood into his veins as the bike began to accelerate. Sue opened it up, and the bike went faster and faster. Soon they were flying. *It felt good to simply be alive*, Delaney thought, *holding onto another decent human being that he could trust completely.* He didn't know how long that would last, and he didn't care.

Epilogue

Upstream

$\mathcal{I}$t was late April when Ed Masterson made his way down to the Charles and went out for his first row of the season. His boat felt heavy and strangely unfamiliar as he carried it out of the boathouse and set it carefully into the water. He fit the oars into their proper locks, clamped down the gates, and ran the seat back and forth along the tracks a few times to test the wheels. Then, collecting the grips in one hand, he carefully lowered himself into the delicate shell and double-checked the footboard screws to make sure that they were tight. Satisfied that everything was secure, he finally shoved away from the dock. The boat slid away, free and clear.

He felt his body give an involuntary shiver as his fingers grazed the surface of the water. It was still quite cold, but he was excited to be out on the river again, getting ready to take his first strokes. Only a month earlier, a thin but persistent layer of snow had lined the banks of the Charles, and deep down the earth still held frozen water. As the days warmed, it would slowly melt into the river. Upstream, just above the dock, Masterson could hear a faint trickle of water, draining out of an overflow pipe near the Eliot Bridge. As he rowed past it, he instinctively looked down into the tea-colored water. He could not see the bottom. The reflection of morning sunlight on the surface of the river made it difficult to see anything deep, but he couldn't help thinking that living things lay below.

On land, red-winged blackbirds had already returned, shifting from branch to branch along the shore, uttering their percussive trills as he passed. He also spotted a pair of hooded mergansers bobbing about, unwilling to leave their winter abode. Other signs of nature were still scant, as if lying in wait for the sun to get stronger. Spring rowing could be dangerous until the water and air temperatures rose to a combined temperature of 90 degrees, and the boat club usually imposed a "four-oar" only rule, which had only recently been lifted. Rowing a single scull was still a bit dicey, and only diehards like Masterson were out. After all, it wasn't unheard of to see a snowsquall, even in April.

Without thinking, Masterson began his warm-up routine as someone in a rowboat might, beginning with short strokes using his arms and back, then slowly adding more and more length by using the sliding seat. The scull responded nicely, gliding forward and picking up speed, and soon he was taking full strokes, settling into an easy rhythm. Masterson was surprised at how quickly his hands and body fell into the familiar pattern of the rowing motion so deeply engrained in his limbs. Soon he was enjoying the magical pleasure of moving across water, and every muscle in his body seemed to take delight in the simple act.

The sobering air of early spring and the absence of other boats on the river allowed him to row without distraction, and soon he found himself going under bridges and past historic landmarks without registering their names or relevance. The river was just the river, with its ever-changing aspects. A bridge was just a bridge to be navigated through. A building was simply a mark to steer by. The further upstream he rowed, the fewer manmade things there were to encounter. He began to take his bearings from trees and rocks, and he noticed the night herons perched along the banks. Soon Masterson lost interest in them as well because they all looked the same. He found himself drifting off into his own thoughts, letting the rhythmic motion of his oars allow him to try and sort through everything that had happened over the past several months.

A woman he had loved had left him and gone off to deceive another, a rich man who had then turned around and killed his own son. It was as simple as that, and now it was over. Still, it was difficult to let it go entirely and to rid his mind of all the disturbing images. He was lucky to have escaped from the whirlpool effect of Finley's death, which had dragged so many other lives down. If nothing else, it made Ed Masterson realize how interconnected everyone around him had been. Connected by water. Still, it felt cleansing to be out on the river again, and free of all the jealousies, self-doubt, and anger.

Stroke after stroke unfolded and quickly disappeared, like the inward swirling puddles of the oars that briefly marked his progress. Far upstream, he finally reached the two marinas that marked the normal end point of navigable river, beyond which lay a narrow stretch of water leading toward Watertown Square. Continuing forward, he now had to turn around more often to spot the half-submerged logs and overhanging branches that could damage his boat or cause him to capsize. But he **knew the way,** and the dense bank of foliage on either side was like a green curtain leading him forward.

After a few minutes of careful steering, he came to a small stone bridge with a single arch, the final point beyond which he could not row. The bridge acted like a funnel for the broader section of river above it, and as he eased his boat forward, under the arch, he felt the arms of the current working against the hull. It gently tried to push him off his centerline, but he held his position. It was dark and pleasant under the arch, and he stayed there for a while, just using his oars enough to hold himself in place, feeling and hearing the moving water rush by him.

The shade of the bridge allowed him to see down into the water more clearly, and he scanned the shallows on either side of his boat. Finally, he spotted the blue-green bodies, moving like luminous spirits underwater. The river was suddenly alive with them, and as his eyes adjusted to the dim light, he began to spot more and more of the s-shaped bodies. They were everywhere now, massing together in the shallows, moving upstream against the current. Suddenly he heard a splash, off to starboard, and then another one off to port.

Once as a kid on Cape Cod, he'd captured a pair of spawning herring and watched their silver bodies lying still in the net. Out of water, they were completely helpless, yet these ancient seagoing fish apparently swam for miles to spawn in the same water where they'd been born. Their tenacity was impressive. As Masterson watched their shadowy forms, they eventually seemed to move as a single mass, driving toward an unseen destination. He wondered if they felt any sense of relief to find their way back home. More likely it was just a compulsive behavior, done to perpetuate the species.

Finley Sparks entered his mind again. He wondered if he would ever not think about him, whenever he was out on the river. Even though Masterson had been exonerated of any wrongdoing, he still felt partly responsible for the boy's death. When you coached people, you took them into your care. Even with the difficult ones, it was a connection that often lasted for life.

Let it go, he said to himself.

There wasn't much room to maneuver under the bridge, where it was shallow and rocky. To turn the boat around might mean damaging it, so Masterson finally let himself drift backward into the pool of water below. A few ducks were floating happily there, in a little eddy that they had discovered. It felt good to stop rowing and do nothing for a moment, just watching the ducks and letting the current carry him. He briefly remembered a Tennyson poem called "The Lady of Shalott" about a woman lying in a boat, drifting downstream as her life ebbed away. There was something about a curse, or a life unfulfilled. He couldn't remember the details anymore, but it made him think about Athena Sparks and wonder what she was doing now.

Let it go, he thought to himself again. Then he spun around and began to row back home.

When he was free of the narrow stretch of river, he finally relaxed and fell back into rhythm, allowing his mind to empty again. The morning sky had clouded over as he headed home, focused on keeping the weight of his body centered over the keel. It was a pleasing sensation, to be perfectly balanced, and to feel the shell move steadily along as he guided his oars forward without touching the water until the moment they caught hold again. Suddenly, he felt a raindrop land on his shoulder, and then another. Then the rain began to break the surface of the water, turning it into a textured canvas. As it soaked into Ed Masterson's hair and body, water began to run down over his face and eyelids. He had to squint, and soon he was nearly rowing blind. He didn't mind. It was a refreshing feeling, rowing in the rain, with the water slowly covering his entire body. He felt alive and moving, rowing with all his other senses. All around him the river was quiet and empty, and somewhere nearby he could still hear the red-winged blackbirds, singing in the trees.

It was going to be a perfect day.

Afterword

The Call of Mystery

$\mathcal{A}$ few years before he passed away, I had the great pleasure of meeting Robert B. Parker, the celebrated writer whose wonderful quote adorns the front of this book. Our meeting came about in a roundabout way. His wife, Joan, had started attending a yoga class I was teaching in Cambridge, Massachusetts, and when she eventually discovered that I was an aspiring young writer with a book coming out, she started chatting with me one day about the tedious necessity of giving author readings for self-promotion.

"Bob really hates doing them," she confided. I nodded and smiled, as if I knew what she was talking about.

Bob? I thought to myself, wondering whom she was referring to and why I should know him. In short order, I solved the mystery, using my trusty Google search engine. Joan Parker's husband, Bob, was none other than Robert Brown Parker, who'd created the famous Spenser detective series. Anyone who had lived in Boston during the late 1980s knew about these from the popular TV adaptation, *Spenser for Hire.*

To be honest, up until that time, I hadn't been a huge fan of mysteries, or at least detective books, outside the typical boyhood fascination with Sherlock Homes and Edgar Allen Poe. My literary aspirations were aimed toward what I thought of as the "high literature" of twentieth-century fiction: Hemingway, Fitzgerald, Orwell, and the like. These were the authors I'd studied in college who were held up as the literati, to be emulated in order to learn the writer's craft. Still, when Joan asked me if I'd like to come over to the house and meet Bob, I immediately jumped at the chance. I ran out to the Harvard Coop to buy my first Robert Parker novel, *Hundred-Dollar Baby,* and devoured it quickly. I wanted to become familiar with some of his writing before I showed up at his doorstep and dared ask him for an autograph. As it turned out, the Parker novel was an easy, fun read, and the story took place right in Boston.

The Parkers lived on Ash Street, right outside of Harvard Square, in a 12-room Victorian that was once described as "something that belonged in San Francisco." Their living arrangements and marriage were also unique. Bob lived downstairs in the classic but quirky old house, and Joan had her own apartment on the second floor. At one point, so the story goes, the Parkers had considered splitting up, when the bloom of romance had begun to wane. But since neither one of them really disliked the other, they'd made the practical decision to continue living together. Separate but equal, they remained good friends.

Bob welcomed me into his study and showed me where he wrote all his novels, at a huge desk that suited his impressive, bearlike physique. Built-in bookcases lined the walls, stuffed with books and photographs. Without any prompting on my part, Parker casually explained that he often worked on two or three novels at the same time, so that he could be more efficient. This seemed mind-boggling to me, like a chess master playing multiple opponents at the same time. But Bob had found it to be a practical approach. After all, you could only take a narrative so far along each day without giving your mind a rest. But if you had three stories going on simultaneously, you could move each one forward a little bit, while you let the other two sit and marinate.

Writing, he bluntly explained to me, was primarily a way for him to support his family without having to resort to an ordinary, humdrum job. He then proceeded to describe how it all worked financially, including specific details about how much he made for each book, the percentage his agent took, and how long he was given to complete them. I'd met other well-known writers before, but none of them had been so forthcoming and honest about the business of making a living as a professional.

One of his dreams was to write more westerns, but he explained that his publisher wasn't keen on them, as they wouldn't make as much money as the detective series. It was all business, he explained, and it wasn't particularly easy; but it was much better than teaching writing—the normal fate that most writers took on as their "day job." Parker himself had taught at Northeastern after getting a PhD in literature from Boston University. He explained how he'd come to resent the time spent teaching others, because it robbed him of his energy to write. So, one summer, Joan supported him as he churned out his first detective novel. The book was a success, and the rest was history. Professor Parker became Robert B. Parker.

As I stood there, taking all of this in, many of my romantic fantasies of what it meant to be a writer started melting away. At the end of the day, writing was a job, just like any other. It made perfect sense, and yet, I'd always wanted to believe that writing was somehow a more glamorous occupation. After all, from the outside, people looked up to writers as literary magicians who could conjure stories out of thin air. Right? Then again, a lot of the sobering truths that Parker was telling me I'd heard before but ignored, like the Hemingway quote, "It's easy to write. Just sit in front of your typewriter and bleed."

In terms of general acclaim and adulation, Bob also cautioned me that writing mysteries wasn't going to gain you any respect from the highbrow university crowd. Then again, few of them ever made a living from their writing. The Parkers lived right on the edge of the Harvard campus, but the divide between their social circle and the high-minded halls of academia was noteworthy. He told me that he and Joan were largely overlooked by the Ivy League crowd, and they couldn't care less.

I left the house with a bundle of signed books in my arms, and a new respect for this warm and unpretentious man. I read all the books he gave me and began to reread other mystery writers, like Dashiell Hammet. One thing was immediately clear to me. These were authors who had economized their writing into tight, descriptive sentences that moved the plot forward without unnecessary embellishment. The story wasn't about them, showing off with their flowery prose, it was all about telling a good story.

Since the passing of Robert B. Parker, the mystery genre has only become more and more popular, expanding its scope and readership. Blockbusters like Stieg Larsen's *The Girl with the Dragon Tattoo* and Daniel Brown's *The Da Vinci Code* have helped draw in a broad range of readers. And of course, the master of mystery and horror, Stephen King, keeps churning out stories that thrill and delight. An essay he wrote in 1981 called "Why We Crave Horror Movies" offered a wonderful explanation for the fascination we all have with death, gruesome or banal: "We make up horrors to help us deal with other ones." It's no surprise, then, that I felt compelled to write *Body of Water* during the days of COVID-19, when I needed a good distraction from all the doom and gloom happening around me.

Body of Water takes place in Boston, and more specifically, on the Charles River, which runs through the heart of the city. Having spent more than half of my lifetime plying this waterway as a rowing coach, I've developed a unique perspective that I've always wanted to share, and this story presented me with the perfect vehicle. I've met many characters along the banks of the Charles, and many of them appear in this book as composite figures. Most people who visit or even live in the city of Boston view the river as a bucolic backdrop to the urban center. But for those who work on the river every day, the waterway is the main stage and everything else around it is the backdrop. In reading *Body of Water,* you'll enter the obsessive subculture of rowing, as seen through the eyes of a Boston state police detective who is a stranger to that privileged world and a rowing coach who is an insider.

Those familiar with Robert B. Parker's work will see that I pay homage to him here, not only with the quote at the front of this book, but in the playful relationship of Sean Delaney and Sue Chasen. Their back-and-forth repartee, as they slowly become involved with each other and solve the crime, was no doubt inspired by the pages of a Parker novel. Supposedly, Parker's wife, Joan, was the model for the character of Susan Silverman, Spenser's girlfriend, who never let the detective get too high on himself. Quite unintentionally, I created a similar figure: a strong and wise woman to help stir the plot.

Another favorite childhood author of mine, Robert Louis Stevenson, once suggested that all good stories were mysteries. I hope *Body of Water* succeeds on both fronts and leaves you feeling at least momentarily delivered from the challenges of living in this all too mortal world.

Daniel Boyne